YESHUA

YESHUA

The King, The Demon and The Traitor
Ancient Mysteries Retold

G.P. Taylor
&
Paula K. Parker

Authentic

First published 2012 by Authentic Media Limited
52 Presley Way, Crownhill, Milton Keynes, MK8 0ES
www.authenticmedia.co.uk

British Library Cataloguing in Publication Data

A catalogue record for this book is available from the British Library

ISBN: 978-1-86024-829-0

Cover Design by Giles Davies
Illustration by Liborio Daniela Festa
Printed and bound by CPI Group (UK) Ltd., Croydon, CR0 4YY

Contents

1

The Birth

The evening fire had lasted long into the night but now its remnants smouldered in the ring of stones. The moon had risen long before and the sky was filled with bright stars. They clung to the canopy of the sky as if they were diamonds sewn onto the velvet of the night.

A small boy, no more than 10 years old, lay huddled in the long cloak that belonged to his older brother. It was wrapped around him, covering all but his sunburnt face and dark eyes. He was alone. Apart from the flock of uneasy sheep the hillside was deserted. Stirring from his sleep as if the whispering wind was speaking to him of his fate, the boy slowly opened one eye and then the other. He was fearful of what he would see.

In the sky above the stars burned brighter than they had ever done before. It was as if they had come to life and moved across the galaxy, pushed by an unseen hand. It was then that he had the sudden and dreadful feeling that all was not well. Where was his father? Where was his brother? Where were the rest of the shepherds? Yet, somehow, the boy knew he was not truly alone. He'd had the feeling before, one night when he was 7 years old. Sleeping on the flat roof he had dreamed that something was staring at him from the darkness. It was only when he awoke from his sleep and opened his eyes that he had seen the snake at the foot of his bed. Its head had been folded back as if about to strike. The long black tongue had flickered in the darkness and then . . . the hand of his father had snatched it around the neck and cast it from the roof. Now, as he lay alone on the hillside in the dark of night with only the ever-brightening light of the stars, he felt the same.

'Do you always sleep so deeply?' the voice behind him resounded. The boy dared not turn. He looked up at the sky, convinced that the heavens were falling as the stars drew closer. *'Daniel – do you hear me?'* the voice asked.

Daniel turned slowly. Whoever was there knew his name.

'Where is my father . . . my brother–?' he asked but his words suddenly stopped. Terror gripped his throat as he looked up at the biggest man he had ever seen. Daniel's mouth fell open as he gasped for breath.

The man threw his head back and laughed. Bright and radiant – wearing a blinding white robe, a long sword in his hand – he loomed above the boy.

'Fear not, Daniel. I will not harm you.'

'What . . .' Daniel began slowly with the only word his feeble mind could think of. He licked his lips and croaked, '. . . are you?'

'An angel – that is what I am – a messenger of the King of Kings and I bring word to you . . .'

The boy-shepherd screamed in terror. With every word that the angel spoke he glowed more and more brightly. It was then that Daniel realized that there was not one man standing before him but a hundred, a thousand, a hundred thousand. They were not stars in the sky but angels that swooped back and forth above his head. He looked around and for as far as he could see, there were angels standing all around him. As if with one voice they all sang, filling the night air. The boy fell back and lay on the ground staring up at the angel who stood over him.

'My father . . .' Daniel screamed, hoping his words would be heard. 'What have you done with him?'

The angel laughed, bent down and then, with one hand gripped around the boy's waist, lifted Daniel from the ground and held him in the air.

'The heavens declare . . . that tonight . . . in Bethlehem . . . the KING is born and YOU . . . will be a witness to HIM . . . !' the angel roared, his words like the howling of a volcano that echoed across the valley and around the mountains. *'Go . . . find your father and your brother . . . they have gone to the town. NOW RUN . . .'* the angel shouted as he put the boy on the ground and nudged him in the back. *'As fast as you can – go . . . quickly . . .'*

Daniel dared not look back. He ran through the parting multitude of radiant creatures that stood around him. As he passed each one, they turned into wisps of silver mist. Daniel ran and ran, tears streaming down his face as the words of the angel echoed through his mind again and again.

'A king . . . the baby . . .' he said over and over again as he ran towards the town on the path he had walked a hundred times. 'Could this baby be our long-awaited Messiah?'

Daniel's mind was filled with thoughts of the *Messiah*. The one YHWH promised through the holy prophets to send, to be the Saviour of Israel. The one who would rescue them from the Romans. The one who would become the King of Israel. Could this baby really be the promised Messiah?

* * *

In the town below, at the back of a small tavern, the elderly landlord tapped on the door of the stable where he kept his animals.

'Congratulations!' The old man paused. 'There are some men – shepherds – who want to see the child.'

Inside, a weary-looking man stood up and moved to the doorway so as not to wake the woman sleeping on a small bed beside a straw-filled feeding trough containing a newborn baby. 'What?' he asked.

'Yosef – wake Miriam . . . a rabble of dirty shepherds just arrived at my house and they stink more than my animals,' the landlord explained. 'They want to see the child. I told them, "No, leave the young couple alone," but when they told me their story, I changed my mind,' he said quickly, his voice rising in excitement.

'Their story?' Yosef asked. 'What happened . . . how do they know we are here?'

'I should let them tell you,' the old man said as he walked away.

'Yosef?' his wife, Miriam, called to him. He crossed the floor and knelt by her, giving her a drink of water. Then he lit the lamp and set it back on the top of a wooden post. 'What is happening?' she asked, her voice still weak with fatigue.

'The owner of the inn said that shepherds have arrived wanting to see our baby.'

Before Yosef could finish speaking there was another knock at the door and the old man stepped inside, followed by six dirty, dishevelled men. They were hesitant and wide-eyed as they entered. Each looked around as if expecting to see more than was before them. When they saw the sleeping baby, they gasped and fell to their knees.

'It is the child!' one of them said.

'Just as we were told,' another agreed.

Yosef and Miriam looked at each other and then at the shepherds.

'Who told you about our baby?' Yosef asked.

The shepherds looked at each other as though uncertain what to say. Finally, the one who'd spoken first turned to them. His words were hesitant. 'An . . . angel,' he whispered. 'We were watching our sheep on the hills nearby. It was like any other night, then all of a sudden a man appeared in the sky. He was *an angel*!'

Suddenly the door burst open as a young boy rushed in and dived into the arms of one of the shepherds.

'Father! He was huge!' Daniel said. 'Taller than Goliath must have been, with a robe that was blinding white!'

'Daniel, please, let me tell the story,' his father said. He turned back to Miriam and Yosef. 'I'm not ashamed to say that we were terrified. We cried out and fell to the ground. This . . . angel . . . told us to not be afraid. Then he said he had good news. "It will be for everyone in the world," he said. "Today, in the birthplace of King David, a *Saviour* has been born. He is the *Messiah*. You will know it is him when you find a newborn baby lying in a feeding trough."'

Daniel pushed free from his father and took hold of Yosef by the hand.

'Suddenly the whole sky was filled with other angels,' the boy told Yosef. 'I have never heard anything like it; it sounded like all of creation was singing. Then they turned and – flew – upwards. This child is the KING . . .'

His father pulled Daniel back apologetically.

'We had to come and see the child they had told us about.' The shepherd peered at the sleeping baby. 'And here he is, just as the angel said.'

2

The Baptism

The day was overcast and cold. Thunder rumbled far away in the mountains that outlined the earth to the Sea of Galilee. A large crowd gathered on the banks of the Jordan River. Some were dressed in fine linen, some in rags. There were even some wearing priestly robes, others the armour of soldiers. They had gathered from miles around, some from the far side of Galilee. All had come to listen to Yochanan, the man with wild curls and penetrating eyes who stood waist deep in the river. While most of the crowd were moved by the words of the young prophet – as many considered him to be – there were those who were concerned that this wild young man might incite a rebellion against the temple leaders or Rome itself.

Yochanan's outer robe – made from woven camel hair – lay on the bank; resting on it were his sandals, a leather belt and a small bag with the food for the day, a token of bread, fish and locusts.

The wild man's eyes flickered across the shamed faces of the crowd.

'Repent. Confess your sinful ways and turn from them,' Yochanan cried out, his voice carrying across the water and over the crowd. 'Come and be baptized; for the kingdom of YHWH is approaching like stampeding horses.'

As he spoke, more people pressed towards the water. The crowd grew with each word, the dust from their approaching feet rising into the heat of the day. Hundreds of people stood with Yochanan's followers and it was obvious many believed the words he was saying. Their faces gave away their hearts as they waited their turn to be baptized. One by one, men and women, young and old, waded out to him. After speaking quietly with each of them, the young prophet would take them by their shoulders and lower them into the water and then lift them back up. With water streaming from hair and clothes, they would open their eyes in rapturous joy.

Yet within the crowd there were others who were not convinced — a group of leaders from the temple in Jerusalem, standing on the bank of the river. They separated themselves from the common people and shivered in self-righteousness, faces hung with pompous expressions. They squirmed in discontent as they shouted to him.

'Yochanan . . . Baptizer! Who are you?' one asked.

'Are you Elijah come back?'

'I am not,' he replied.

'Are you the Messiah?'

'No.'

'Then who are you?'

'I am one sent into the wilderness to call people to right-eousness, to make the paths straight for the Messiah.' Yochanan pointed to them. 'You low-life, self-serving snakes!' he yelled. 'Why are you here? If you are here to be baptized, then show evidence of your repentance. And don't think that being children of Abraham makes you better than others.' He pointed to the rocks on the riverbank. 'YHWH created man from the dust of the earth; he is able to turn those stones into children of Abraham.'

One of the priests stepped forward. 'You are not a priest,' he sneered as he pointed at him with a hooked finger. 'You say you are not Elijah, nor the Messiah. By what authority do you call people to repent and baptize them?'

'I baptize with water to symbolize the cleansing from the old, sinful life,' Yochanan replied. 'But there is One who will come soon; I will not be worthy to even untie His sandal. He will baptize with the fire of YHWH.'

As if they were one man, the temple leaders turned away and walked through the crowds.

'If the priests are not good enough, then what must we do to please YHWH?' one man asked.

'Care for each other more than you care for your possessions,' Yochanan said. 'If you have two coats, give one to someone who has none. If you have extra food, share that as well.'

A man in a rich coat stepped forward. 'What about me?' he said, 'I am a tax collector.'

'Do not cheat the people by taking more than you are supposed to,' Yochanan replied. 'And repay those you have cheated.'

A temple guard standing in the crowd hesitated and then moved forward. 'What about me?' he asked. 'What must I do for YHWH to accept me?'

'Don't harm anyone. Don't use your power to accuse anyone falsely. Be satisfied with what you are paid.'

While Yochanan continued to preach, a young man walked through the crowds and waited his turn to wade out to the Baptizer. He looked like any other man of his age. His hands were scuffed and calloused with work, his brow dark-tanned from days in the sun. Bright eyes stared out from under his brow and as he waited he pushed back the strands of long hair with his fingers. After several minutes, Yochanan looked up to see the young man standing in front of him.

'Yeshua . . . my cousin . . .' he cried. 'You came. Have you at last heard from YHWH?'

Yeshua nodded. 'I have heard,' he said as he left his sandals on the bank and stepped into the water, 'and I've come to you to be baptized.'

'Why? I don't understand why you are here,' Yochanan said. 'In all of our thirty years, I have never known you to do anything wrong. You don't need to be baptized; in fact, I should be baptized by you.'

'Do it . . . do this now,' Yeshua smiled at his cousin. 'For me, this baptism is not a confession of sin. For me, this symbolizes that my life is dedicated to serving YHWH.'

Yochanan looked at him for a moment and then nodded. Taking his cousin's shoulders, the young prophet lowered him into the waters of the Jordan River. As he lifted Yeshua up, the wind began to blow, swirling upwards to push the clouds away. Thunder rumbled in the mountains and the river water shimmered. The sunlight hit the river, causing the droplets streaming from Yeshua to glint, gem-like. The crowd fell silent. As Yochanan watched, the light around Yeshua intensified, quickly growing into a blinding radiance. Above his head came the beating of wings as if a giant bird hovered over the water. He looked up and saw a dove fly down and rest on the shoulder of Yeshua. Yochanan stood dumbfounded as once again thunder boomed through the clear sky.

'*This is my Son*,' Yochanan heard a voice echoing through the thunder. '*I love Him and am pleased with Him.*'

Yochanan stared wide-eyed at Yeshua, who stood with his eyes closed and his face lifted upwards. He was *different*. It was as if the sunlight still rested on him. It was as if the sunlight came *from within* him. Yochanan whispered. 'You are *He*. You are the *Messiah*.'

As the thunder rolled into the distance, the bright light faded and the water stilled.

Yeshua lowered his face and opened his eyes to look at his cousin. 'I AM,' he said. Turning, he waded to the riverbank and walked up the hill that led towards the wilderness.

Yochanan lifted a trembling hand to point towards Yeshua. 'Look at Him!' he cried to the crowds, his voice echoing across the water. 'Look at the Lamb of YHWH who will take away the sins of the world.'

3

The Temptation

Yeshua walked towards the wilderness, the water streaming from his clothing leaving a trail behind him. His gaze was locked on the path in front of him; when he turned, it was without looking around, as if taking in his surroundings was unnecessary. A long strand of wet hair lay across his forehead. It crossed his brow like the points of a crown. Then, without hesitating, face set like flint, he left his old life behind and walked quickly with determined steps towards the hills and the desert.

The wilderness of Judea was vast and arid. The ground was rugged and the mountains carved out of rough reddish-brown rock streaked with layers of white. Sparse trees and shrubs offered occasional relief from the unrelenting heat and drew what wildlife dared live there: leopards, hyenas, eagles and stray sheep. Each creature drank while watching the others, some fearfully, some with a raging thirst.

Sheltered in the dark shade of a rocky overhang, the great black cobra lay curled up, dozing in the heat. Nearby a rat stroked its whiskers and watched the snake. The rat shuddered and began frantically scratching its ears, shaking its head in misery.

'What is going on?' the rat whined.

The snake opened its eyes. '*HE* is coming,' it hissed.

The rat hunched its shoulders and jumped, looking all around. 'Where? How do you know?'

'Just like you, I can *sense HIS* presence,' the snake replied, 'but unlike you, in this *form*, I cannot react to *HIM* as you do.'

The snake slithered from the shade of the rock. While the rat watched, the cobra began to transform. The black scales split, exposing a pure white skin. The body and head began pulsing as it changed from a slender reptile to the form and countenance of a man, only tall like a giant. Slitted eyes gazed from a face crowned with waves of glistening white hair. The creature stretched – scraps of black skin blowing away in the wind – and smiled, exposing two sharp fangs between blood-red lips.

'Ah, Wormwood,' the creature said. 'Am I not the most beautiful in all creation?'

'Yes, Lucifer, you are.'

'And yet, *HE* still cares for these pitiful humans enough to take the form of one. I kept hidden, meaning to strike in secret, but it did not happen. I was not able to destroy the mother, nor was I able to use that fool Herod to kill the infant. Thirty years have passed and now *HE* is a man. Our time grows short; if I am to rule, I have to try a more *direct* approach.'

Wormwood scurried to the edge of the hill to peer into the valley below. 'What will you do?' he asked, scratching his cheek with a paw.

Lucifer crossed to stand beside the rat. 'Since *HE* was . . . *baptized* . . . *HE* has been in this wilderness – forty days without eating; *talking* with the Creator. I would think by now *HE* would be hungry.' His smile was slow, ripe with a deadly evil. 'I was successful in tempting the first man and woman. Those fools gave in to the suggestion that the Creator did not care for them, that *HE* did not want the best for them. That *suggestion* has worked on these pitiful humans for millennia since then; I have no doubt it will work again today.'

The sound of gravel under footsteps drew his attention. '*HE* is nearly here. Quickly, Wormwood, go; leave this to me.'

The rat scurried to squeeze between several rocks.

Lucifer glanced down at his body, glistening pure white in the sunlight. 'Ah, I must hide my beauty once again.' The brilliance of the skin dimmed, taking on muted flesh tones, the fangs disappeared and eyes softened to the shape of almonds. His size reduced to that of a mortal. With a snap of two long fingers, a robe clothed his body and sandals shod his feet. 'I must appear like one of them,' he smiled to himself.

Turning, he walked back to sit on the rock. Snapping his fingers again, a basket with a scattering of breadcrumbs appeared at his feet. He smiled. 'I am ready,' he whispered to himself, wiping his hands in satisfaction.

Yeshua reached the top of the hill and paused to catch his breath. Dust covered his clothing and – from beneath the covering of his head cloth – his face glistened with sweat.

'You look weary,' Lucifer said from the shadows.

Yeshua looked up to scrutinize the stranger. 'I am,' he admitted.

Lucifer moved over to one side of the rock. 'Please, share my resting place.'

Yeshua sat down and, opening the water skin slung over his shoulder, took a deep drink.

'Your face is gaunt,' Lucifer observed. 'Have You eaten?'

Yeshua shook his head; there was something about the man that he recognized. It was as if he had known him since the beginning of time.

Lucifer lifted the basket at his feet. He pinched some crumbs between long fingers; the air filled with the aroma of warm bread. 'I've just finished eating. I'm sorry I have nothing left to share.'

'I don't need anything now,' Yeshua said, closing his eyes to rest.

'Truly?' Lucifer turned his head slightly to study the weary young man. 'Ah . . . I understand. You are *fasting* – going without food in order to focus on prayers – is that right?'

Yeshua nodded, his stomach cramped with hunger, the pain so intense he could think of nothing else.

'How long have You been fasting?'

'Forty days.'

'So long?' Lucifer commented, arching a finely pointed brow. 'Few in history have fasted so long. Moses, Elijah, special men who were called by . . .' his mouth twisted, '*YHWH*,' he spat out the Creator's name.

'So, Lucifer,' Yeshua said, opening his eyes, 'you find it *difficult* to speak my Father's name. Did you really think to fool me?'

Lucifer's eyes widened in sudden surprise. 'Ah, my dear Yeshua . . . so that is what *HE* has told you during these forty days,' he said. 'And as You know who I am, there is no reason to maintain this . . . boring . . . disguise.' Within a breath, in the twinkling of an eye, he transformed back to his angelic appearance. 'Since You know me, let us talk about *You*. You call *HIM* "Father". That must mean You consider Yourself to be *HIS Son*?'

Yeshua did not respond to Lucifer's transfiguration, nor did he answer the creature's question.

Watching this 'human' sit calmly before his glorious self enraged the creature. Knocking aside the basket of crumbs, Lucifer sneered, 'If You are *HIS* Son, then prove it!' He pointed to the rocks at their feet. 'You're hungry; speak to these stones and command them to become bread.'

Yeshua's gaze was calm. 'It is written in the Holy Scriptures, "Man will not live only on bread, but on the words that come from the mouth of *YHWH*." I will not do something My Father has not told me to do,' he replied. 'He called me to this fast and I will continue to fast until He commands me to stop.'

Rage contorted Lucifer's face. Stretching out a white, muscular arm, fingers extended, he flicked his wrist and suddenly they were no longer in the wilderness, but standing on the pinnacle of the temple. Far below them were the streets of Jerusalem.

'According to the prophet Malachi, "The Lord you are seeking will suddenly come to his temple."' Lucifer swept a hand, indicating the crowded streets below. 'All those people are expecting the Messiah to come in a glorious way – riding on a white horse at the head of an army – to free them from the Romans. Why don't You . . . throw Yourself from this pinnacle? After all,' his mouth twisted again, 'the *Holy Scriptures* state, "*HIS* angels will protect You and keep You from even hurting Your foot."'

'My Father will protect me,' Yeshua replied. 'Just as He is doing even now.' The wind blew through his clothes and whipped at his hair yet Yeshua seemed unconcerned with the danger. 'But the Holy Scriptures also state, "Do not test YHWH."'

Lucifer snarled, his fangs glinting in the sunlight. Another flick of his wrist and suddenly they were standing on a mountaintop. Outstretched before them was the whole world. From horizon to horizon, they could see every nation. 'Look at all the kingdoms of the world,' he said with an insolent gesture. 'There is Rome,' he said, pointing to the west. 'The Roman Empire is the greatest the world has ever known. And next to it is Greece. And over there,' he pointed towards the south-west, 'is Egypt. They enslaved Your people for four hundred years. Wouldn't You like to make them . . . *pay* . . . for what they did to the Hebrews? You can do that now.'

Lucifer swept his arms wide in a grand gesture. 'All these kingdoms – all these and more – are *mine*. All their power and their entire splendour belong to me.

'Your people expect the Messiah to overthrow all their oppressors and return Israel to the golden years of King David's rule. You can do that now. I will give them to You, to do whatever You wish to them . . . *if* . . . You will bow down and *worship me*.'

For the first time since speaking with Lucifer, Yeshua was enraged. He breathed hard as he looked at the demon, his fists clenching with anger. 'Get away from me, you devil!' he commanded, pointing a finger at the creature. 'Even if I have to die, I will never follow you. I will never worship you. For the Holy Scriptures command, "Worship YHWH and serve only Him." Now *be gone*!'

Yeshua flung out his hand and Lucifer stepped back in fear. 'I will go,' he snarled, 'but this is not over between us. We will meet again.'

Lucifer lifted both hands above his head as if grabbing the sky. At once, the winds whipped around him, throwing dust and debris into the air. A dark shadow swirled around him like a summoned tornado. It scattered the pebbles at his feet – sounding like the chattering of a million people. When they settled, the creature was gone.

'*Son of the Almighty Creator?*' a voice echoing like thunder spoke behind Yeshua. He turned to see two men. Like Lucifer, they were taller and larger than any human. Their eyes were a colour not of this earth. Although the wind had settled, hair like lions' manes whipped around their foreheads. Their robes made the sunlight appear dim and wings like an eagle's rose from behind their shoulders.

They knelt, extending their hands. One of these . . . *angels* . . . carried a golden basket filled with bread and the other held a golden goblet, beaded with condensation.

'*For the One beloved by the Creator,*' the angels spoke in unison, '*all needs will be provided.*'

4

The Twelve

The wind rippled the water where the Jordan River flowed slowly into the Sea of Galilee. A group of men stood on the stony beach as they watched the sun sinking slowly towards the horizon.

'Yochanan,' Andros said, 'this is my brother, Shimon.'

The two men were several years older than the Baptizer. They were taller than him – Shimon slightly bigger than Andros – and they both had the rough-hewn build of men who worked outdoors. Their arms were knotted with muscles and brows burnt from working in the sun. But the brothers' countenance marked the difference in their demeanour: while Andros looked upon the world with peace and acceptance, Shimon's gaze was wary and defiant.

'Welcome, Shimon,' Yochanan said. 'Andros has told me of you.' He indicated some men standing with him. 'I understand that you too are a fisherman like my kinsmen Yochanan – who shares my name – and Yaakov.'

Shimon nodded. 'I am.'

'They tell me that you work with them and their father, my Uncle Zebedee. My mother once told me that Zebedee is a shrewd businessman.'

'He is,' Andros agreed. 'But he is also kind and generous. When we moved from Bethsaida to Capernaum, Zebedee offered to help us get started as fishermen.'

'That is indeed kind,' Yochanan replied as he picked a stone from near his feet and rubbed it in his fingers. 'Tell me, Shimon,' he asked, 'have you come to be baptized?'

Shimon's eyes widened in surprise at the unusual question. 'Baptized?' he asked, not knowing why Yochanan had asked the question.

'Yes,' the Baptizer said impatiently. 'To confess the wrong you have done and be washed clean of your past. To prepare for the *Messiah.*'

The big man shook his head. 'Andros and I have heard of the Messiah all our lives. At one time, I believed he would come and free Israel from the power of Rome and restore her to the glory of the kingdom of David. Now I do not know if I still believe.'

Yochanan's eyes blazed in anger. 'Believe!' he said, jabbing a finger at Shimon. 'YHWH's kingdom is closer than you know, but not the kingdom you think. Confess your evil ways!'

Shimon's hands balled into fists. 'Are you saying that I am evil?' he said as his eyes narrowed into slits.

Andros grabbed his brother's arm and pulled him away from the Baptizer. 'Come on, Shimon,' he said. 'We must go. Remember, we promised Ruth to be home for the meal on time.' He looked over his shoulder. 'I'll be back tomorrow, Yochanan,' he called.

'Did you hear what he said to me?' Shimon fumed as they walked back towards Capernaum. ' *"Confess your evil ways!"* ' he mocked. 'If he dares to say that to me again, I'll . . .'

'You'll do what?' Andros asked. 'Hit a prophet of YHWH? Shimon, you always act first and think later. Yochanan speaks the truth of YHWH and, if he says the kingdom of YHWH is coming, then I believe him. Now, what do you think Ruth and her mother have prepared? You might not care for your wife's mother, but you cannot deny that she is a good cook.'

Shimon found it hard to eat. The words of the prophet echoed around his mind. He couldn't hear the quibbling of his wife or her mother. He sat outside throughout the meal, looking at the burning embers of the cooking fire. When he laid down to rest, sleep did not come to him and he was glad when it was time to go to work that night.

Around midnight, he joined the other fishermen by the boat and they put out to sea. They fished all night, throwing and hauling in their nets as the waves rocked back and forth like the thoughts in his head.

As the sun rose and they put back to shore, Shimon could think of nothing else.

Andros climbed out of the boat and waded to shore holding a net that contained their small catch. 'Shimon, I'll take these to Ruth, and then I'm going to see the Baptizer.'

'What do you mean, you're going to see the Baptizer?' Shimon asked. 'We still have work to do. There are nets to mend.'

'Don't you remember? I told the Baptizer I'd go back this morning after we finished fishing. Yaakov wants to come too.'

Shimon looked over at Zebedee, who was talking with his sons. 'You're going to let Yaakov go before the work is finished?'

Zebedee nodded. 'Let them go. There's not much left to do here; then I'm going to find a shady spot and take a nap. If Yaakov and Andros want to stand around listening to the Baptizer instead of sleeping, well . . .' he spread his hands, shrugging his shoulders at the crazy notions of younger men.

'Go on,' Shimon waved his hands towards his brother. 'But don't think you can get out of mending nets every day.' He watched Andros and Yaakov run towards the road as excited as young boys, and then reached down to pick up a net that had got tangled. The muscles in Shimon's arms bulged as he tugged at a knot in the net, but it refused to loosen. Giving up, he threw it down with a curse and picked up another net from the bottom of the boat.

'Problems with the nets?' Zebedee asked. The older man was standing on the shore, spreading his nets out to dry.

'My net got twisted as I pulled it in,' Shimon said. 'If I cannot untie it, I will have to cut it and mend it.'

'Like I tell my sons, Yochanan and Yaakov, YHWH sends a tangled net to fishermen to teach them patience.'

'I don't have time for patience.'

Laughing, Zebedee waded out to the wooden boat, removed the net from Shimon's hands and put it in the boat. 'It will be easier to untangle when the net is dry,' he said. 'Secure your boat and go home to your wife. You have been fishing all night. A full belly and sleep will ease your frustration.'

'I cannot go home!' Shimon paused and then sighed and stood to face the older man. 'I am sorry, Zebedee,' he said. 'It is not the net. I am worried about the catch. It has grown smaller each week. What will we do when there is nothing left?'

'We will do what we have always done,' the older man said. 'We will trust YHWH.'

Shimon laughed. 'You sound like my brother and that *Baptizer*,' he said. 'I cannot *wait* for something to happen; I will *make* it happen.'

'And you sound like my sons,' Zebedee laughed, slapping the younger man's shoulder. 'You three are all wind and waves and storms. Here, grab the other end of the boat.'

Together they pulled the boat out of the reach of the lapping water. Made from cedar and oak, it was curved like a sliver of the moon and capped with a single sail hanging from a mast in the centre of its 8-metre length. At more than 2 metres wide, it was big enough to carry more than a dozen men. Grabbing the thick rope tied to the end of the boat, Shimon wrapped it several times around a large rock.

By the time they finished, the morning sun was pinking beyond the hills on the far side of the sea. Zebedee and

Shimon paused to gaze at the tranquil surface of the water lit with shades of orange, red and gold from the rising sun.

'The sea is so beautiful,' Zebedee whispered.

'Beautiful, yet deadly. Winds can whip between the hills on either side of the sea and turn those peaceful waters into a violent, dangerous storm in an instant,' Shimon said.

'Yet you love it,' Zebedee said, throwing an arm around the younger man's broad shoulders. 'Nothing will ever call you away from this life, Shimon. Once a fisherman, always a fisherman.'

'Not always,' Shimon muttered as he walked away from Zebedee and sat under the shade of a large tree and looked out across the water. *Why can I not rid my mind of his words?* he asked himself as he thought of the prophet.

Shimon closed his eyes. The sun warmed his body and he slept through the day.

That evening, when the net was dry, Shimon was able to untangle the knotted cords and pick out the long strands of dried weed. While he was rolling it up to store in the boat, he heard someone running towards him. Turning round, he saw his brother.

'Shimon! Shimon!' Andros stopped when he reached the shore, bending over to catch his breath.

Shimon ran to grab his brother's arm. 'Andros? Is something wrong?'

The other man straightened and shook his head, 'Nothing is wrong. In fact, everything is *wonderful*. I have seen *him!*'

Shimon's brows lowered in confusion. '*Him?* Who are you talking about?'

'I've seen the *Messiah!*' Andros's eyes were shining with excitement.

Shimon dropped Andros's arm and took a step backwards. 'The Messiah? You've seen the Messiah?' Shimon asked.

Andros nodded.

'What do you mean?'

'Yaakov and I were with the Baptizer this morning. We were helping with the people who had come to the Jordan to be baptized. Suddenly, he points towards the top of the hill and says, "Look! There is the Lamb of YHWH!"'

'I turned and saw the man Yochanan was pointing to; he was walking along the road. There was *something* about him that drew me. Without thinking, I began following him. I had climbed to the top of the hill when I realized that Yaakov was doing the same.

'This man turned and saw us following. He stopped and waited for us; when we caught up, he greeted Yaakov – apparently they are related – and then asked us what we wanted.

'I looked at Yaakov and then asked the man, "Teacher, where do you live?"'

'He said, "Come and see."'

'We followed him and talked with him all day until about an hour ago. Now we need to go.'

'Go?' Shimon asked. 'Go where?'

Andros shook his head as he gabbled his words like an excited child. 'Go to *him!* You've got to meet him.'

Shimon scratched his head. 'Andros, I don't know . . .'

Andros grabbed his arm and began pulling him down the road. 'No!' he insisted. 'You must come! He wants to meet you. Come . . . come quickly.'

A short time later, Shimon was standing in a nearby house while Andros introduced him.

'Teacher, Yeshua – this is my brother, Shimon.'

For a moment, the young man looked at Shimon intently. Then he smiled and grasped Shimon's forearm. 'Shimon, your name means "he has heard". But now you will be called *Cephas.*'

'Cephas?' Andros said, laughing. 'That means *rock*, doesn't it? That fits Shimon. He can be as hard-headed as a rock.'

* * *

Several more days passed and the brothers' catch continued to dwindle. 'We've got to catch *something* soon, Andros,' he said. 'We have to.'

That night, the sea was calm; the conditions were perfect. Shimon 'Cephas' looked at the still waters. 'A perfect night to catch a net full of fish,' he whispered to himself.

Throw after throw – the net always came up empty. By the time the clouds were reflecting the first rays of the morning sun, a dispirited Shimon Cephas and Andros, together with Zebedee and his two sons, Yochanan and Yaakov, were pulling their boats up the beach.

While they were cleaning their nets, Shimon Cephas saw Yeshua walking along the water's edge, followed by a large group of people. The people were crowding the man, almost pushing him into the water in their desire to listen to what he had to say.

Turning, Yeshua saw the fishermen and walked up to them.

'Shimon Cephas and Andros, good morning to you. Good morning, Zebedee, Yochanan and Yaakov.' He smiled as he talked, his eyes looking as if they knew all of their secrets. 'Shimon Cephas,' Yeshua said, staring him in the face, 'would you take me out a short distance from shore? It would make it easier for me to teach these people.'

Before Shimon Cephas could open his mouth, Andros said, 'Certainly, Teacher. Get in.' Shimon Cephas sighed and stood to untie the rope and push the boat back into the water.

After they had drifted a few yards out, Yeshua told them to stop. He turned towards the shore and began teaching, his voice echoing across the water.

While the Teacher spoke, Shimon Cephas mended a net and listened. Yeshua's voice – deep and rich – resonated across the water. He spoke the same message as the Baptizer: of the need to admit wrong acts and live a godly life. But there was something more: he spoke of YHWH *loving* all people. Shimon Cephas had never heard that from any of the teachers at the synagogue.

The big fisherman felt strangely drawn to this young man with his dark skin, bearded jaw and tangled hair. Looking at the crowds standing on the water's edge listening intently to the Teacher, Shimon Cephas could tell they felt as he did. By the time Yeshua had finished and sat down in the boat, the sun was halfway up the morning sky.

Looking over at the brothers, Yeshua said, 'Sail into deeper water and throw your nets out for a catch.'

Shimon Cephas opened his mouth but, when he saw Andros's pleading eyes, he swallowed the sharp words. Taking a deep breath, he spoke as if talking to a child, 'Teacher, I do not know what trade you learned, but it is obvious that you are not a *fisherman*. We fished all night – which all fishermen know is the best time – and we caught *nothing*. However, since it is *you*, we will do as you ask.'

Yeshua watched as Shimon Cephas and Andros raised the sail. When the boat was in deeper water, they lowered the sail, lifted the nets and threw them overboard. Then Shimon Cephas sat down, folded his arms and smiled at the teacher, who smiled in return.

Suddenly Shimon Cephas felt the boat twitch, then jerk, and then rock as the rope from the net sank into the depths as if yanked by the hand of a giant. He jumped up to grab the rope, while Andros jumped up to grab the other rope. Hand over hand, they started heaving on the ropes and when the nets broke the surface of the water they were filled with dozens of fish. The water bubbled with frantic fish trying to escape. The wood of the boat creaked under the weight of the nets.

'Zebedee! Yochanan! Yaakov!' Shimon Cephas called to their friends on the shore. 'Quick! Come and help!'

A few minutes later, their friends' boat pulled up alongside. Grabbing the edge of the net, they hauled it onto their boat. Together, the two boats dragged the net, filled to the brim with fish, to shore. As the fishermen laughed, calling it the largest catch they had ever had, Shimon Cephas looked at the Teacher, who continued to smile.

Dropping his end of the net – much to the dismay of the other men – Shimon Cephas fell to his knees in front of Yeshua.

'Please leave me, Teacher! The Baptizer was right; I am a man of evil ways. I don't deserve to be in your presence.'

Yeshua reached out to put a hand on Shimon Cephas's shoulder. 'Don't be afraid of me,' he smiled. He looked at the men in the two boats. 'You have caught fish all your life. Come with me; from now on, you will catch men, women and children for YHWH's kingdom.'

Yochanan and Yaakov looked at their father. 'Go,' he said, giving a nod.

'Truly?' Andros said. He looked at his brother. 'Shimon Cephas?'

Shimon Cephas looked at Yeshua and then climbed out of the boat to wade to the shore. Turning back he waved a hand at the others. 'Come on!' he said, 'What are you waiting for?'

* * *

Just as Shimon Cephas followed, so did others. They grew in number, first his closest friends – twelve in all – and then more disciples. Every one leaving their jobs to listen to the teacher. Late in the year they journeyed to where the family of Yeshua lived.

'Mother! Joses! Juda! I see him!' Shalom called, looking out the front door. 'Yeshua is here. And he has a group of men with him!'

Miriam hurried from the other room, just as her eldest son entered the house. 'Yeshua!' she cried, hugging him. 'It's been so long since I last saw you.'

'I have missed you too, Mother,' Yeshua smiled. He turned and greeted his sister and younger brothers.

'And you've brought guests,' Miriam said. 'Invite them in.'

'These men are my good friends and disciples.' He laughed. 'Some people call them "the Twelve".' Turning, he introduced the men who followed him as they walked through the door, bowing to Miriam and Shalom.

'This is Shimon, but I call him Cephas.'

'Greetings, Cephas, welcome to our home.'

'Thank you.'

'This is Andros, his brother. And Philippos, Netanel, Levi (he was a tax collector before he joined us), Taoma (who is a twin), Yaakov the younger (I'll explain why we call him "the younger" later), Thaddai, another Shimon (who is a Zealot) and Juda (who takes care of our money).' As the last two men entered the door, Yeshua added with a smile, 'And I think that you know these two.'

'Yochanan! Yaakov!' Miriam cried. 'My nephews! How are you? It has been so long since I last saw you.'

'We are well,' Yochanan said.

'Now, all of you please sit and rest,' Miriam said. 'Shalom, please offer your brother and our guests some goat's milk. I am going to make some sweet honey cakes for supper.'

As they sat around the table in the centre of the room, Miriam lit the candles and said the Sabbath prayer. When she had finished and they had all eaten, Yeshua's brother Juda looked at him.

'So, brother, will you be teaching tomorrow at the synagogue?' Juda asked. 'Everyone has heard how you are a famous teacher like our cousin, Yochanan the Baptizer. Some even say they've heard that you've *healed* those who are sick.' It was obvious from the questioning tone of his voice that Yeshua's brother wasn't one who believed that report.

'If the leader of the synagogue wishes it so, I would be honoured to teach,' Yeshua answered knowing the heart of his brother.

Cephas leaned against the wall by the window. In his hand he held a cup of wine. He wanted to grab Juda the brother of Yeshua and shake the disbelief from him.

The next morning Yeshua and his disciples followed his family into the synagogue. All of the people in the village greeted him, patting him on the back, commenting on how long it had been since they had seen him and how they had heard wonderful things about him. When the leader of the synagogue asked him to present the teaching, Yeshua nodded. The elderly man reverently carried the scroll that contained the Holy Scriptures and kissed it before handing it to Yeshua.

Yeshua stood and unrolled the scroll. After scanning the writing for a moment, he began reading words by the prophet Isaiah:

'YHWH's Spirit is on me, because he has anointed me and called me to preach good news to the poor. He has sent me to proclaim freedom to the prisoners and to tell the blind they will receive their sight again; to release those who are oppressed by Lucifer and to announce that YHWH is ready to bless all those who come to Him.'

Yeshua rolled up the scroll, kissed it and handed it back to the synagogue leader. Then he sat down and bowed his head in prayer.

Everyone in the room looked at him, waiting to hear what he would say about Isaiah's words concerning the Messiah, the one who would rescue them from Roman oppression and would become the King of Israel.

After a few minutes, he looked at the people. 'Today,' Yeshua told them, 'this Scripture is fulfilled in your presence.'

Gasps rippled through the room followed by the murmur of angry whispers.

'What did he say?'

'Did Yeshua just say that the prophet Isaiah was speaking of him?'

'Who does he think he is?'

'This is Yeshua, the carpenter, Yosef and Miriam's son.'

The buzz grew until the synagogue leader stood and gestured for everyone to calm down.

He looked at Yeshua and said, 'Is that all you are going to say? Do you not wish to explain your words? We've all known you since you were a child and now you're trying to declare you are something more?'

Yeshua stood and looked at the crowd.

'I know you are going to quote the old proverb, "Doctor, heal yourself". You want me to do miracles like those you have heard about. You have to *see* something before you will believe, because you *think* you know who I am,' he sighed. 'Just as with Joseph, Moses and Elijah – and many other prophets of old – no prophet is accepted in his home town.'

The room erupted in a firestorm of anger.

'Are you saying we are stupid?' a man shouted.

'Do you think you are the Messiah?' asked another.

Standing, Yeshua gestured to his twelve disciples and they left the building, with his mother and family following.

'Yeshua! What have you done?' his brother Juda demanded. 'Did you just announce to the whole village that you are the promised *Messiah*?'

'But, he . . .' Cephas started to speak, but stopped at a quiet gesture from Yeshua.

'You know me, Juda,' Yeshua said to his brother. 'Who am I?'

Juda stared at his oldest brother for a moment and then threw his hands in the air. 'What do you mean, who are you?

You're my brother – maybe you're a little tired and saying crazy things – but you're *just* my brother. Who do *you* think you are?'

Yeshua looked at Juda and then his other brothers, then his sister. He shook his head and turned to his disciples. 'Come, it is time for us to leave.'

'Yeshua,' Miriam said. 'You are– '

'No, Mother,' he smiled sadly at her. 'Not now – I must go. The kingdom of YHWH is coming like a stampede and I must go and preach to those who will believe.'

5

The Wedding

'Cana isn't usually so empty,' Netanel said, as he led Yeshua and the other disciples through the streets of his home town.

Cephas clapped him on his shoulder. 'Well, it isn't every day that a wedding takes place,' he said. 'I hope there is food and drink left by the time we arrive.'

'Daniel and Anna's wedding celebration goes on for another four days,' Netanel laughed. 'No one runs out of food or wine by the third day.'

'Well, if it takes us much longer to arrive,' Andros smiled, 'the wedding feast will be over.'

Netanel frowned, hitching his bag on his shoulder. 'I can't help it if I do not remember locations easily,' he said.

'But you *grew up* here,' Andros said.

'Do not worry,' Yeshua said, clapping a hand on Netanel's arm. 'We have arrived. The wedding is over there.' He pointed to a large house at the end of the street.

The disciples gaped wide-eyed at the Teacher. 'How did you know where the wedding was taking place?' Cephas asked.

Yeshua smiled, 'If the flowers placed around the doorway were not an indication, the music and laughter coming from the large number of people in the house and courtyard would let everyone know a wedding celebration was being held there.'

The disciples burst into laughter and turned to walk the short way up the street. Flowers, woven into long garlands, were draped around the door to the house; nearby, a small table stood in the partly shaded courtyard. The men stopped near the door, where six large stone jars stood; each held water used for ritual cleansing. After washing their hands and the dirt from their feet, the men brushed the dust from their robes and hair.

'Yeshua! You are finally here.'

Turning, the men saw the Teacher's mother standing in the doorway of the house, holding a pottery cup. She set the cup down on the small table and hurried to her son. She was frowning.

'Yes Mother, we are here,' Yeshua said. 'I'm sorry we missed the ceremony. We were . . .' he glanced at Netanel, '. . . delayed in our journey. But there is still time to celebrate Daniel and Anna's wedding.'

'It isn't that,' Miriam said, wringing her hands.

'What is it?'

Miriam looked first at the disciples and then back at her son. She gestured for them to follow her a few steps away from the noisy celebrations. Making sure none of the wedding guests were nearby, she leaned in to whisper, 'There is no wine left.'

The disciples gasped. 'Oh no!' Andros said. 'How embarrassing.'

'It will be considered an insult to all the guests,' Netanel said.

'Daniel's mother is my friend,' Miriam told the disciples. 'She said they did not consider that the weather would be this hot, nor that extra guests would come from outside Cana.' She looked at her son. 'You must do something.'

'Me?' Yeshua asked.

'Yes, you,' Miriam insisted. 'You've known Daniel and Anna all your life. Daniel's mother is as close as a sister to me.'

'Why me?'

Miriam sighed, 'All the other guests are inside,' she explained. 'They know nothing about the wine. If anyone from the wedding left to buy some wine, someone might suspect something.' She looked at her son. 'No one knows you and your friends have just arrived. You can do something and no one would know.'

'Mother, you know I care about Daniel and Anna,' Yeshua said, 'and would not want to see their wedding ruined nor have them embarrassed.'

'I have some money,' Netanel said. 'It's not much, but I would be glad to offer it, if it would help.'

'Cephas and I have some money as well,' Andros said.

'Where would we buy wine?' Cephas asked.

Netanel sighed. 'It won't work,' he said.

'Why?' Cephas asked.

'Is the wine merchant at the wedding?' Netanel asked Miriam.

She nodded. 'Yes, in fact he is the steward of the wedding.'

The disciples groaned.

'Well, we could go to the next town,' Andros said, 'but it would take time to buy the wine and bring it back here.'

'That would take too long,' Miriam said. 'By that time, some of the wedding guests would know.'

'What would you have us do?' Yeshua asked his mother.

'Yeshua, *listen to me!*' Miriam grasped his arm, '*You* must *do* something, son,' she insisted.

'Mother,' he gently removed her hand from his arm, '*I* must *do* only what YHWH tells me to do,' he said. 'I will listen to *no one else.*'

His mother's eyes widened and she looked at her son for several moments. Finally, she nodded. 'I understand,' she whispered.

Yeshua looked at her for a moment and then closed his eyes. 'Father,' he whispered, 'what do You want me to do?'

Turning, Miriam walked back towards the house. She stopped in the doorway and gestured towards someone standing inside; a moment later, two men – one much shorter than the other – appeared. From their simple robes, it was obvious they were servants helping at the wedding.

'Yes?' the taller servant asked. 'Do you need something?'

Miriam pointed towards Yeshua. 'Do whatever he tells you to do,' she said and stepped across the threshold into the house.

The servants crossed to Yeshua and his disciples. Yeshua didn't move. They shifted their feet, glancing from Yeshua – who was still praying – to the disciples. Not wanting to disturb the Teacher's prayers, the tall servant raised a questioning eyebrow; Cephas shrugged in response. They all looked at Yeshua, who remained as he was for several more minutes.

Finally, he opened his eyes and looked at the two servants. 'Fill the water jars,' he said.

The servants frowned, looked at each other and then back at Yeshua.

'Sir?' the taller one asked.

The Teacher pointed towards the six large jars near the house. 'Those jars,' he said. 'Fill them.'

The shorter servant tugged on the sleeve of the tall servant. 'I didn't hear clearly,' he whispered into his ear. 'I thought he said to fill the jars.'

'He did,' the tall servant whispered over his shoulder.

'Why? How much wine has he consumed?' The short man asked. 'He must be drunk. What do we do?'

'Do?' the tall servant said. 'Whatever he tells us to do; just like the lady said.'

'But fill the jars?' the short man was incredulous. 'Not all the jars are empty. All the guests are here. Even if others arrive . . .' he glanced at Yeshua and the disciples '. . . there is still plenty of water in the jars. I do not think there is a need . . .'

The tall servant spun round and grabbed the short man's shoulders. 'You were not hired to *think*,' he spat. 'You were hired to serve the guests of the wedding. We were told to fill the water jars and I will see to it that we fill them *to the brim!* He shoved the shorter man towards the jars. 'Now, get moving.'

The taller servant turned to bow to Yeshua, 'It shall be done as you ask,' he said and followed the other man.

The two servants picked up two smaller jars that stood nearby and walked past Yeshua and the disciples towards the centre of the town, where the well was located. After several minutes, they returned, carefully carrying the jars so as not to spill the water. Emptying the water into the first of the six large jars, they returned to the well. After several trips, each of the six jars was filled to the brim with water.

The servants put their jars down and turned to bow to Yeshua and the disciples. 'How else may we serve you?' The taller man asked.

Yeshua picked up the cup his mother had left on the table. 'Dip this into one of the jars,' Yeshua said, 'and carry it to the steward of the wedding.'

The tall man looked at the cup in Yeshua's hand and shook his head. 'Please forgive me, sir. It has been a long day and I don't think I heard you correctly.'

Yeshua put the cup into the man's hand. 'Dip this cup into one of the jars,' he said slowly, as if to a child, 'and take it into the steward of the wedding.'

The tall man looked at the cup and then at Yeshua. 'What should I tell him, sir?'

'Tell him nothing,' Yeshua replied. 'Just give him the cup.'

The tall man looked at the other servant, who smiled smugly at him. Straightening his shoulders, the tall servant bowed to Yeshua. 'It shall be done as you wish.' Turning, he crossed to the tall water jars and dipped the cup into the one nearest the door. Without looking at his companion, he went to find the steward of the wedding.

The shorter servant stood still for a moment, until Cephas cleared his throat. Startled, the man jumped and, eyes opened wide, gave a hasty bow and ran after his companion.

Cephas burst out laughing. 'That was hilarious!' he said, bending over to slap his knee. ' "Fill the jars with water." "Take a cup of the water to the steward of the wedding." Teacher, I think *both* of those men thought you were drunk.'

The other disciples started laughing.

'So, what about the wine, Yeshua?' Andros asked. 'What should we do?'

'Do?' Yeshua smiled and turned to walk into the house. 'I'm going to join the wedding feast.'

His disciples stood frozen for a moment and then hurried after him.

The room Yeshua entered was crowded with the wedding guests. Some sat near low tables laden with platters piled high with bread, cheese or meat and bowls filled with olives and dates. Other guests sat near one end of the room, where the bride and groom, Anna and Daniel, along with their parents, brothers and sisters, were seated. The steward of the wedding – a good friend of the groom's family – was sitting close by. It was his responsibility to oversee the wedding feast, especially the serving of the food and drink.

'Yeshua!' Many in the room called greetings to the Teacher. Yeshua waded through the crowd, speaking to one here, nodding to another there. As he approached the groom's table, Daniel looked up.

'Yeshua!' the groom cried, standing to embrace the Teacher. He waved to the other disciples who stood nearby. 'Netanel, Andros, Cephas, I began to wonder whether you were coming.'

'I would never disappoint you, my friend, by not showing up at this most important moment in your life,' Yeshua said. 'Congratulations, Daniel and Anna. May YHWH bless you with many years of love and may children fill your home with joy.'

'Thank you, Yeshua,' Daniel smiled. 'Thank you.'

'Sir,' the tall servant was standing near the steward of the wedding; in his hands was a small cup.

The steward looked up at the servant. 'Yes?' he asked.

The servant began to offer the cup and paused when he saw Yeshua and the disciples standing next to Daniel. He looked at Yeshua, who nodded. Taking a deep breath, the servant extended the cup to the steward.

'Ah,' he said, taking the cup, 'time to serve the next wine.'

The servants – and the disciples – opened their mouths

to warn him, but stopped at a glance towards Yeshua. Each man bit his lip as the steward lifted the cup to his mouth. Each one closed his eyes – grimacing in distaste – as the steward began drinking.

'*Ahhhhh* . . . that was . . . *amazing!*'

The men's eyes popped open to see the steward of the wedding stand and walk over to Daniel. He threw an arm around the groom's shoulders.

'It is tradition for the best wine to be served first at a wedding,' he said. 'Later – when the guests have had too much to drink, you serve wine that has been watered down. But you,' he said, hugging Daniel's shoulders, 'you have saved the best until now.'

'You!' the steward said, turning to the two servants and lifting his cup. 'Serve this *perfect* wine to the guests. Hey! Wake up!' he said, snapping his fingers in front of the servants' shocked faces. 'What's the matter? Is there only a small amount of this wine?'

'Ahh . . . n-n-no,' the tall servant stuttered. The colour drained from his face as he glanced at Yeshua. 'There's . . . *plenty* of *that* wine.'

Yeshua turned to walk towards a table and passed his disciples who stood with their jaws dropped, gaping at the cup the steward held. 'Come,' the Teacher said, 'let's join in the celebration.'

6

The Questions

'Teacher?' Cephas said, shaking Yeshua by the shoulder until he woke. 'Wake up.'

Yeshua rolled over on the low bed, shielding his eyes against the flickering lamp his disciple carried. 'What is it Cephas?'

'There is someone here to see you.'

'In the middle of the night?' Yeshua asked as he sat up, rubbing his eyes. 'Who is it?'

'It is *Nicodemus*,' the disciple whispered in awe. 'Even though my home wasn't in Jerusalem, I have heard of him. Besides being a Pharisee and a member of the Sanhedrin – the ruling council – it is said his family is one of the wealthiest in the land.'

Yeshua smiled. 'Then show him in, Cephas,' he said as he tossed aside the blanket and stood up to pull his tunic over his head and slip on his sandals. He had just finished tying his robe when Cephas ushered a man, his face hidden by a hooded cloak, into the room.

'Greetings,' Yeshua said. 'I am Yeshua ben Yosef.'

The newcomer lowered his hood to reveal a man older than Yeshua, with thick dark hair, a full beard and eyes that gazed at the Teacher as if unsure whom they saw.

'I am Nicodemus ben Gorion,' he paused. '*You* are the one that the Baptizer referred to?'

'Yes, he is,' said Cephas, who had left the room and returned to put a tray with flatbread and cheese on a low table.

Andros followed his brother with a jug of goat's milk and two cups. 'He is the Messiah,' he said.

Yeshua waved a patient hand at his disciples.

'These are two of my followers, Cephas and Andros; they are brothers.' The three men nodded at each other in mute greeting. Yeshua smiled as the two brothers bowed and left the room. 'They are good and loyal men,' he said, offering his guest a cup of milk. 'But you did not come to see me in the middle of the night to speak of my disciples.'

Despite rich clothing that proclaimed his wealth, position and power, Nicodemus appeared hesitant and shy. He chose his words carefully.

'Teacher,' he began, 'we – some of the members of the Sanhedrin – we know you have been sent by YHWH. We have heard of the *miracles* you have performed; no one could do these if YHWH were not with him.' He paused to look at the other man.

Yeshua said nothing and nodded for Nicodemus to continue.

'We have heard there are many who consider you to be the Messiah who will restore Israel and the kingdom.'

'What do you believe?'

Nicodemus lifted his hands as he shrugged.

'I do not know. Many believe the Messiah will restore an earthly kingdom to Israel, but certain Holy Scriptures imply it will be *YHWH's kingdom.*' He smiled briefly, 'I would like to see that.'

'Nicodemus,' Yeshua said, 'no one can see YHWH's kingdom unless he is born again.'

The guest frowned in confusion. 'Born again? What do you mean? Surely you're not suggesting that a grown man can be born a second time?'

Yeshua sighed as he broke some flatbread in two and handed a piece to Nicodemus. 'I am not talking about human birth. I am speaking of spiritual birth.'

'I don't understand,' Nicodemus said reaching for a piece of cheese. 'How can this happen? This is not possible.'

'You are one of Israel's teachers. You have studied the law and the prophets and yet you do not understand? You know from the Holy Scriptures that YHWH can change a man inside – change his spirit, heart and soul – and make him into a new person.

'The prophet Ezekiel said that whoever is cleansed by YHWH will have a new heart and a new spirit; an obedient spirit that will do whatever YHWH commands. This is what I mean.

'You say that you and others in the Sanhedrin know YHWH has sent me. You say that you have heard of the things YHWH has given me power to do. But you do not understand what I am saying and you do not believe. Yet it is through belief in the One YHWH has sent that men and women will receive spiritual life that will never end.'

'What?'

Yeshua reached over to lay a hand on Nicodemus's forearm, his gaze penetrating deep within. 'YHWH loves this world so very much that He sent his beloved Son and, if anyone believes in Him, he will never experience spiritual death, but will live forever. YHWH did not send His Son to condemn the world, but to save it. Whoever believes this will not be condemned, yet those who do not believe are already condemned because they do not believe in YHWH's Son.'

'Condemned? Nicodemus faltered.

Yeshua stood and crossed the room to look out of the window at the night sky.

'The Messiah is the "Light" that has come into the world, yet men love the darkness because it hides their evil deeds. Those who live by YHWH's truth will come into the light.'

Turning away from the window, he gazed at his guest. 'You came here, Nicodemus, because you wanted answers to your questions. Now I will ask you one question: *do you believe?*'

Nicodemus paused, his hands folded on his knees, his brows furrowed in thought. After several minutes, he looked up at Yeshua and . . . smiled. 'I believe.'

* * *

The next morning, Cephas and Andros were openly curi-
ous about Nicodemus's visit, but as the other disciples
were around, they refrained from asking Yeshua about his
midnight visitor. Yeshua smiled as if he knew their
thoughts and said nothing about his conversation with
Nicodemus.

'Let's go to Galilee today,' Yeshua said over a simple
breakfast of bread and fresh goat's milk.

'Galilee?' Philippos asked. 'Why do you wish to go
there?'

'Because YHWH wants me to take His message of the
kingdom to the people there.' He took a drink from his cup.
'We will go through Samaria.'

That comment drew a response from his disciples that
was far from the message of love Yeshua taught.

'Samaria!' Cephas spat. 'Those pigs.'

'They're not true Hebrews!' Yochanan said. 'If we touch
them we will be unclean.'

'Samaritans hate us as much as we hate them,' Thaddai
said. 'They will attack us if we go through their land.'

Yeshua stood, the smile gone from his face.

'YHWH created *all* people,' he said, 'and He has sent me
to preach the good news of His kingdom to *everyone*. Hatred
has no part in what I have come to do. Do not speak this
way to me again.' He looked at each of his disciples; one
by one, they dropped their heads in shame, murmuring

apologies. 'You are forgiven,' he said. 'Now, get ready to leave.'

By midday, they had reached Sychar, a town near a well that their ancestor Jacob had dug. Yeshua sat in the shade of a rock placed over the well.

'I am fatigued,' he said. 'We should rest here and eat.'

'Eat!' Cephas clapped a hand against his forehead. 'In our haste to leave, we forgot to buy food.'

'There is a village over there,' Andros said. 'We could go and buy food there.'

'I am not going to buy food from—' Cephas clamped his mouth shut at a quick glance at Yeshua. He nodded. 'Let's go. Teacher, you stay here and rest.'

Yeshua adjusted his head cloth to shade his face, leaned his head against the rock and closed his eyes. Several minutes later, the sound of rock moving against rock drew his attention. He sat up and looked around.

A woman stood on the other side of the well. She was in her middle years and, although she had once been a beauty, she looked old and worn. A large jar and a leather bucket attached to a long coil of rope were on the ground near her.

She was removing the flat rock that covered the opening to the well. Once she shifted the rock, she lifted the bucket and rope and wrapped the end of the rope around the rock covering and dropped the bucket into the well. After several seconds, a splash echoed up the well. She began pulling on the rope and, after a moment, the bucket – filled with water – appeared at the top. She poured this water carefully into her jar and set the bucket down to cover the well again.

'Hello,' Yeshua said.

The woman screamed, almost knocking over her water jar as she turned round. She grabbed the bucket once more and held it in front of her as if it were a weapon.

'Do not be afraid,' Yeshua said. 'I will not harm you. Would you let me have a drink? I am very thirsty.'

The woman's expression changed from fear to scorn.

'I can tell from your accent that you are a Hebrew,' she said. 'I am a Samaritan. I am surprised you would ask me for anything, even a drink of water.' Unlike most women, she had no problem speaking with a strange man. She stood straight and looked Yeshua in the eye, although she still held the bucket close.

'If you really knew who I am and knew of the wonderful gift YHWH has for you, you would ask *me* for living water.'

The woman looked doubtful. 'How could you get this *living water*?' she said, setting the bucket down and folding her arms in front of her. 'You do not have a rope or a bucket and this well is very deep. Besides, are you saying that you are greater than our ancestor Jacob? He dug this well for his family and for their animals.'

Yeshua smiled, knowing her heart. 'Ah, but after drinking from this well, you will soon be thirsty again,' he said. 'If you drink from the *living water* I speak of, you will never be thirsty again and it will give you a life that will never end.'

The woman looked surprised and her expression changed from scorn to excitement. 'Then please give me some of that water,' she said. 'Then I would never be thirsty again and would not have to come to this well every day.'

'I will gladly give this water to you,' Yeshua said. 'Go and bring your husband and I will give it to both of you.'

The woman's appearance – that moments before had been excited and expectant – now looked dejected. Her shoulders drooped, her cheeks were washed with colour and she stared at the ground.

'I– I do not have a husband,' she whispered.

'That's true,' Yeshua said gently. 'In fact, you've had five husbands and the man you're living with now didn't want to marry you.'

The woman's eyes had been wide when Yeshua first started speaking to her; now she gawped disbelievingly at him.

'Sir,' she gasped, 'you must be a prophet! You knew about me and . . .' She paused, as she realized *what* this prophet knew about her. Her face flushed from her hair to the neck of her robe. Her eyes shifted back and forth as she thought furiously. After a moment, she lifted a hand to point at a nearby mountain. 'If you are a prophet,' she said, 'then tell me why you Hebrews claim that Jerusalem is the only place to worship YHWH but our leaders tell us that our ancestors worshipped at Mount Gerizim?'

Yeshua smiled as if he knew that she was trying to guard her thoughts and heart from him. 'A time is coming,' he said, 'when no one will be concerned whether you worship YHWH on Mount Gerizim or in Jerusalem. It is not *where* we worship Him that matters, but *how* we worship: whether that worship is spiritual and real. YHWH's Spirit helps us in this; for He is spirit and we need His help to worship Him as He wants. You Samaritans worship blindly without knowing Him. We know all about Him, for He has sent salvation to the world through the Hebrews.'

'What you say may be true,' the woman said, 'but I do know one thing. I know that when the one they call the Messiah comes He will explain everything to us.'

Yeshua looked at her for a moment. 'I am the Messiah.'

The colour drained from the woman's face and she opened and closed her mouth in shock. Her hands were shaking as she took hold of the rope from the bucket and held it tightly.

She didn't notice the two men approaching.

'Teacher, we're back,' Cephas said, as the disciples approached carrying baskets filled with bread and cheese.

It was Levi who first noticed the woman and nudged Thaddai with an elbow. One by one, the disciples stared at the woman, who was staring at Yeshua as if an angel had appeared before her. After a moment, she dropped the bucket and turned and ran from the well, leaving her water jar behind.

The men watched her for a moment. Finally, Andros turned and spoke to Yeshua.

'Here, Teacher, we brought some food,' he said. 'The merchants didn't have much right now; the harvest is four months away. But, the bread is fresh and the cheese is quite good. While Taoma draws water from the well, sit down and eat.'

Yeshua looked at his disciples. 'I have food you don't know about,' he said.

The disciples glanced at each other.

'How did he get food?' Juda asked. 'I am in charge of the money.'

'Do you think that woman gave him something to eat?' Netanel asked.

Yeshua shook his head. 'I receive the food that gives me life when I obey YHWH and complete the work He has sent me to do.'

Cephas arched a suspicious eyebrow at Andros who shrugged in reply. 'Teacher, we do not understand what you are saying.'

The Teacher sighed. 'You say that the harvest is still four months away.' He stood and pointed in the direction of the village. 'Look around you. There are many fields of human souls that are ready to be harvested and YHWH will reward those workers who reap those souls for His kingdom.'

Yochanan walked up to him. 'Yeshua, come and sit down,' he said. 'Eat.'

The disciples ate in silence. Everyone wondered what Yeshua had talked about with the woman but no one wanted to ask. As they were wrapping the uneaten food to carry with them, Yaakov pointed in the direction of the village. 'Look,' he said.

They all turned to look at the road. The woman was returning, followed by a large group of villagers. She walked up to Yeshua.

'I believe . . . you are *Him*,' she whispered. Turning to her companions, she said, 'This is the man I told you about. He knew all about me and told me everything I ever did. He has to be the Messiah!'

One of the village men walked up to Yeshua. 'Sir,' he bowed his head respectfully, 'I am Ahron, a leader in the village. This woman said some . . . amazing . . . things about you. We would like to hear what you have to say for ourselves.' He turned to indicate the other villagers. 'We would be honoured if you and your followers would stay with us.'

Yeshua placed a hand on the man's shoulder, causing everyone to gasp. 'May YHWH bless you for extending kindness to strangers.'

7

The Demoniac

'I don't like this time of night,' Taoma whispered, stumbling on a large rock as they left the boat and walked across the shore. 'It's neither complete night nor full day.'

Thaddai nodded, 'My father's mother always told me that evil spirits roamed freely during this time.'

The two men, at the back of the Twelve following the Teacher, looked around nervously. The shoreline that Yeshua led them along was narrow, the lake's water – black in the twilight – on one side, lapping at their feet as if tasting them. On the other side – barely discernable against the waning night – tall cliffs with jagged edges loomed treacherously over the lake. The wind groaned around the cliff walls like a lost soul. Taoma and Thaddai looked at each other and then quickened their steps to catch up with the others.

Walking around the end of the rock wall, the men found themselves in a small canyon-like cove. The howling wind grew stronger, whipping around the canyon as if trying to break free. A rocky path sloped along the cliff walls past caves and large boulders.

'Tombs,' Taoma shuddered. 'Those caves are tombs.'

A wild scream drew their attention to the slopes of the cliff. Silhouetted against the sky, stood a man with massive arms raised in challenge. He screamed again, a guttural sound that was more animal than human. Turning, he scrabbled down the cliff, pausing only to pick up several large rocks to throw at them. One rock landed near Taoma; he gasped and jumped back. It was not a rock; it was a human skull.

The disciples backed away as the shrieking monster approached them.

'He's huge . . . a monster,' Andros said, 'like Goliath.'

'He's crazy,' Levi said.

'He's not crazy,' Thaddai gasped, 'he's a demoniac; he's possessed.'

In thirteen long strides, the giant ran up to Yeshua. The man was taller than any of the Twelve, dwarfing even Cephas. Filth caked his skin and hair, and the tattered shreds of rags hung on his body. His hair was matted, with large patches missing, as if pulled out in clumps. His eyes bulged as if to burst from their sockets; in the light of the moon, they appeared to glow red. Lengths of broken chains hung from his limbs. Lifting a large rock over his head with both hands, he screamed curses at the disciples.

The Twelve turned and ran, stumbling into each other in their haste.

'Stop!' Yeshua commanded.

The disciples froze. Slowly, as if fearful of being noticed, they turned to see Yeshua facing the crazed giant holding the massive rock.

The man screamed, his massive jaws contorting, spit frothing over broken teeth. Falling to his knees, the giant dropped the rock to pick up a long sharp stone near him. He jabbed the point into his chest. Blood spurted as he pulled the stone out and jabbed himself repeatedly.

'Stop!' Yeshua pointed at the demoniac.

The giant threw the sharp stone down. Lifting his head towards the sky, he opened his mouth. Without moving his jaws, voices – hissing, roaring, guttural voices – poured forth.

'What do You want with us, Yeshua?' the voices from within the demoniac asked.

'Come out of him,' the Teacher said.

The demoniac fell to the ground, writhing and scream- ing, clawing at his torso; his body bulged and rippled as if multitudes of beetles and snakes were crawling beneath his skin. He rose to his hands and knees, arching his shoulders and retching.

'Stop!' Yeshua commanded, 'Evil spirits, you . . . come out of him.'

The demoniac opened his jaws again.

'What do You want with us,' the voices hissed, 'Yeshua, Son of YHWH? Promise us by . . .' the man retched again, 'the *Almighty* . . . that You won't torture us.'

The man screamed and jumped upright. Grabbing the longest length of chain from around his waist with both hands, he snapped it as easily as if it were a piece of string. He lifted the chain, looped one end around his neck, and began pulling on the other end. His eyes bulged and his face darkened, but he continued to pull. Opening his mouth, the voices roared, 'Why do You care about this insect of a man? No one else does.' The chain tightened. 'Do not send us out of this area into the abyss. Promise us, or we will kill him.'

'Stop now!' Yeshua commanded.

The demoniac's hands opened and the chain dropped from his neck. He dropped to the ground, writhing and gasping for air.

The Teacher pointed towards the demoniac. 'What is your name?'

'Name?' the thousands of voices screamed. 'We don't have *one* name; we have many names. Our name is Legion, for we are many. We did not kill this insect. Promise us . . .' The demoniac lifted his hand, still shaking from his close brush with death, towards the nearby cliff. 'Look,' the voices snarled, 'there is a herd of more than two thousand pigs on that hill. If we leave this man, let us go into them.'

'Go!' Yeshua replied. 'YHWH will deal with you.'

The wind swirled around Yeshua and the man; it screamed as it lifted the demoniac above the Teacher's head. The demoniac hunched and gagged, as if trying to vomit out his very soul. Dropping the man near Yeshua's feet, the wind whipped up the side of the cliff to surround the herd of pigs.

Squealing in rage, the pigs attacked each other, kicking and biting. As if with one mind, the herd turned and ran towards the edge of the cliff, jumping and leaping from the edge towards the dark waters of the lake below.

The Twelve, frozen to the spot by the sight of Yeshua confronting the demoniac, looked up to see thousands of pigs plummeting towards them. They jumped back against the base of the cliff's rock wall, just as the pigs began hitting the water.

The disciples stared at the pigs, which, instead of trying to swim to safety, continued attacking each other. Deafeningly loud squeals gradually diminished as, careless for their safety, the pigs thrashed about in the water until one, and then another, sank into the depths of the lake below.

'What was in him?' Cephas asked, unsure of what he had seen.

'A legion of demons,' Yeshua answered as he bent down and comforted the sobbing man. 'Now he is free from them.'

Shortly afterwards, the swineherds came running along the shore followed by other men from the town.

'That's him! That's the man.'

Yeshua turned to see a group of about twenty people carrying torches and lanterns approaching them.

'Are you looking for me?' Yeshua asked.

One man, dressed in a rich robe, stepped forward.

'I am Mahali. I am one of the elders of the region of Gerasenes.' He gestured towards someone in the crowd, a scrawny man with a broken nose. 'Hiram is a swineherd; he and his men told us a . . . an unbelievable story.'

'It isn't unbelievable,' Hiram hunched his shoulders and pointed at Yeshua. 'We were on top of the cliff with our herd. I – we – saw this man kill the demoniac and then destroy our pigs. Look!' he pointed towards the lake, where carcasses floated. 'There are the pigs. Do you believe me now?'

The elder turned back to Yeshua. 'The destruction of so many pigs is a serious matter,' he said.

Cephas leaped to his feet. 'Yeshua didn't *kill* anyone!' he said. 'He cast a legion of demons out of the man.'

'No man has ever been strong enough to subdue the demoniac,' Hiram sneered. 'We've bound him with chains many times and yet he always broke them.'

'Hiram, you will be quiet or you will leave!' Mahali said. 'Sir,' he said to the Teacher, 'Hiram is right; there is a demon-possessed man that lives among these tombs. Have you seen him?'

'Yes,' Yeshua answered. 'He's right here.' He gestured to a man sitting on the shore. Wrapped in the Teacher's outer robe, was a large man with lengths of broken chain trailing from his body.

Several people in the crowd stepped back in fear.

'That can't be the demoniac,' one man said.

'It looks like him,' another said.

'But this man is not crazed,' a woman said.

'I was with the men who tried to chain him,' said another man, 'and those are the chains we used.'

The man seated near Yeshua stood up. 'I am Othniel; I am – I was – the demoniac,' he said. 'Yeshua cast the demons out of me.'

People in the crowd gasped and stepped even further away.

'Sir,' the elder said, 'this is wonderful.' He hesitated. 'Did you . . . *do something* . . . to the herd of pigs?'

'Yeshua didn't hurt the pigs,' Cephas snapped. 'The demons left the man and possessed the pigs. They went mad and jumped off the cliff.'

The crowd whispered furiously among themselves, but none kept their voices low.

'Two thousand pigs destroyed?'

'I can't afford to lose my herd!'

'I can't afford to lose mine either.'

'First our pigs, then what? Will he drive demons into our other animals? Into our families?'

'He's got to go.'

'Are you going to tell him?'

'Me? No! He might attack me as he attacked the demoniac and the pigs.'

'Someone has to tell him.'

'Mahali, you tell him.'

'Me?'

'Yes, you're our elder. You tell him.'

The crowd turned to face Yeshua. Hiram and several others nodded to him. The elder licked his lips, took a deep breath and stepped forward. He held his hands out pleadingly.

'Sir,' he said, 'we mean no disrespect, but please . . . leave. Our herds are our money.'

'Leave?' Cephas said. 'The Teacher cast demons from this man and healed him – and all you can think of are *pigs*?'

'Cephas,' Yeshua laid a hand on the disciple's arm. 'I shall go.' He looked at the crowd. 'I'll not stay where I am not wanted.'

The Teacher turned and began walking back along the shore of the lake; his disciples followed.

'Yeshua!' Othniel ran down the shore to fall at the Teacher's feet. 'I don't want to stay with these people. Please let me come with you.'

Yeshua grasped the man's arms and lifted him up. 'No,' he said. 'You cannot come with me. You must stay. Soon these people will lose their fear of you and want to hear your story. Then you can tell everyone what YHWH has done for you.'

Othniel breathed deeply and then nodded. 'I will do as you ask. I will tell them that YHWH sent you, Yeshua, to save me and heal me. And if *I* can be healed, then *anyone* can be healed.'

8

The Leper

'Teacher, look at all the crowds,' Shimon said, sweeping his hand towards the people following Yeshua and his disciples down the road. 'One word from you and they will stand against the Romans. At last we will throw those *dogs* out and return Israel to the glory of King David's reign.'

'Shh, Shimon,' Taoma hissed, looking over his shoulder. Several people in the crowd were trying to walk closer to Yeshua. 'I know you used to belong to the Zealots but you can't keep thinking of ways to overthrow the Romans. If they heard, you would be arrested. And us as well, just for being your friends.'

'No one in this crowd talks to the Romans,' Shimon dismissed Taoma with a wave of his hand. 'Besides, I'm not worried. I still have connections with the Zea– with others who wish to see the Roman rule gone. One word,' he snapped his fingers, 'and I could get swords and men ready to fight.'

'And you think that is what I want?' Yeshua asked. 'Shimon, have you not listened to my teaching? I am here to establish YHWH's kingdom on earth.'

Shimon shook his head in confusion, 'But, Yeshua, isn't that what I just said? The prophet Samuel said that King David was a man who sought after YHWH's heart. If we restore Israel to the glory of King David's rule, wouldn't that be bringing this kingdom you speak of?'

Yeshua shook his head, sighing. 'Shimon, you have much to learn about me and my Father.'

'Hey! Get away from here!' A voice from the crowd screamed.

Yeshua and his disciples stopped walking and turned round.

Behind them, people were yelling and moving away from something in the midst of the crowd.

'What are you doing here?'

'Get away! You don't belong here!'

'Throw some rocks! That will make it move!'

Whatever it was, from the shifting of the crowd, it was moving towards Yeshua. Soon, someone scuttled out from the centre of the crowd. Dressed from head to foot in torn rags, it was impossible to tell whether the person was a man or a woman. That didn't matter to the people in the crowd or the disciples; the torn rags – and the person's cry, 'Unclean!' – revealed something far more vital.

'A leper!' a woman screamed. The area around the rag-covered creature opened up as the crowd – and the disciples – jumped back.

The leper lifted a trembling hand and removed the rags draped over its face to reveal a man. The lack of wrinkles suggested he was still young, yet every inch of his body appeared to be rotting. Skin white as bleached bones was covered with sores: some crusted, some swelling, some oozing pus. There were many bald patches on his scalp, and any of the filthy hair that remained on his head and in his beard had turned white.

Leprosy was a death sentence. According to the Law given to Moses, anyone afflicted with the disease was to live the rest of his life apart: separated from his family, separated from his friends, separated from the rest of society. Until the day he died, a leper would never again feel the touch of another human.

'He shouldn't be here!' a man yelled. 'He's unclean.'

'Get out of my way!' a woman cried. 'I don't want to touch him and catch leprosy too.' The woman turned and ran down the road with the crowd following behind her.

Ignoring the screams of the crowd as they ran towards the town, the leper stumbled across the road and fell to his knees in front of Yeshua.

'Teacher, move away!' Cephas yelled from the safety of the far side of the road.

Yeshua ignored Cephas's cries and stood looking at the pitiful man kneeling in front of him.

'Please . . .' the leper began to weep. 'Please, sir, please help me.'

'Why should he help you?' Shimon said. 'He's a righteous man. You must be a bad person for YHWH to punish you with this disease.'

The leper sobbed into the dirt. 'Please,' he begged, 'help me.'

'How long have you had leprosy?' Yeshua asked.

Filthy hair brushed the road as the leper shook his head. 'I do not know,' he wept. 'I have lost count of the years.'

'Do you have a family? A wife? Children?' Yeshua asked.

The leper nodded. 'My wife and I had two sons and a daughter. My daughter was but a babe when I was struck with this disease. For all I know, she is a grown woman.'

The leper straightened up and clasped his hands towards Yeshua. 'I want to be with my family again,' he said. 'Please, sir, if you are willing,' he begged, 'please heal me. Make me clean.'

Yeshua reached out to place a hand under the man's chin; the leper melted under the feel of the Teacher's hand. Lifting the man's face, Yeshua gazed into his eyes.

'I am willing,' Yeshua smiled. 'Be clean.'

The man's breath caught in his throat, his eyes widening. Lifting his trembling hands in front of him, the leper watched the skin on his arm ripple as wounds dried and scabs fall as flesh began knitting back together. The man dropped his hands to grasp the neck of his ragged tunic. Ripping the cloth, he exposed a chest that was changing from bone white to the colour of healthy tissue.

The man looked up at Yeshua, 'I'm healed,' he whispered. Jumping to his feet, he shouted. 'I'm healed!' He began capering about on the road, dancing and laughing, 'I'm healed! I'm healed! I'm healed!' Turning to Yeshua, he dropped to his knees once again. 'How can I thank you, sir? I don't have much left, but whatever I have, I will give it to you.'

Yeshua reached down to place his hands under the man's arms and lift him up. 'I don't want your things,' the Teacher said. 'I just did what my Father told me to do. Now, you must obey the Law of Moses. Go and show yourself to a priest. Once the priest confirms that you are healed and cleansed of leprosy, then go, offer your sacrifice of thanksgiving to YHWH.'

9

The Teachings

'Cephas, you are a blessed man,' Yeshua said excitedly with a broad smile, throwing an arm around his disciple's shoulders. 'Ruth is not only a godly woman, but a wonderful cook.'

'Thank you, Yeshua,' Cephas answered. 'I know she will be pleased to hear that. I do not know which she enjoys more; preparing meals or having guests.' The big fisherman laughed. 'Since having guests means cooking, either way she is content.'

Yeshua took a deep breath. 'It's a magnificent morning,' he said as he looked towards the horizon. 'Let's walk up the mountain together. I would like to spend some time in prayer.'

For a while, the two men walked in the comfortable silence of close friends. When they reached the mountain-top, they stopped and looked at the vista.

'Teacher, I know you grew up in Nazareth,' Cephas said, 'but I do not believe there is anywhere as beautiful as the hills around Capernaum.'

Yeshua nodded. 'It is beautiful.' From where he and Cephas stood, they could see the fertile Plain of Gennesaret, with brightly coloured wild flowers dotting its lush green grass. Far below were the blue waters of the Sea of Galilee.

'This is a good place to come and pray,' he said. 'It not only has beautiful scenery, it is a quiet and solitary place where I can be alone with my Father.' He pointed to a large rock under a shady tree. 'I will go over there to pray and give you privacy for your prayers.'

The fisherman watched the Teacher walk to the other side of the mountaintop and kneel by a rock. After shifting his feet and looking around, Cephas finally shrugged and found a rock to kneel by. Glancing over at Yeshua, he leaned against the rock and clasped his hands. Checking his position with the Teacher's once more, he leaned his head against his hands and closed his eyes.

'Uh . . . Almighty YHWH?' Cephas began. 'I . . . uh . . .' he took a deep breath and then rapidly recited the *Shema*, a traditional prayer he had learned as a child, 'YHWH is our God, YHWH is one . . .'

He took another breath and opened an eye to peep at Yeshua; the Teacher was still praying fervently and it did not appear he would finish soon. Cephas sighed; *I am a simple fisherman*, he thought, *not a priest. I don't know how to spend hours praying.* He tried to think of something more to pray about but the combination of a full stomach and the gentle breeze blowing across him was more than he could handle.

Cephas's breathing slowed, his hands and head dropped ever closer to the rock and soon he was snoring.

'Cephas . . . *Cephas* . . .'

A foot nudging him startled the fisherman. 'What?' He sat up, staring wide-eyed at Yeshua, who stood over him. Tilting his face, he covered his mouth with his hands and subtly wiped the drool that had trickled out. He stood.

'I'm sorry, Cephas,' Yeshua said. 'I did not mean to disturb your prayers.'

'Well, that's all right,' Cephas blustered and then glanced at the Teacher, who was smiling. He sighed. 'I'm sorry, Teacher. I fell asleep.'

'I know.'

'I've been a fisherman all my life,' Cephas explained, 'and we fish at night and sleep during the day.'

'And now I have changed all that.'

Cephas grasped Yeshua's forearm. 'I'm not complaining,' he said. 'I have never felt more . . . *alive* . . . since following you. You have taught me so many *amazing* things about YHWH – things I had never known before. I've seen *miracles*: you've healed sick people, you've commanded demons to leave people alone, and they *obeyed*.' He dropped his hands, stared at his feet and shrugged. 'I just can't seem to be still and stay awake at the same time.'

Yeshua grasped Cephas's shoulder.

'You make prayer too difficult,' he said. 'Talking with YHWH is like talking to me or to anyone else; it is a sharing of thoughts. You talk *and* you listen.'

'Yeshua! Cephas!' They turned to see Andros waving at them as he walked up the mountain's slope. When he reached them, he said, 'There are people to see you, Teacher.'

'Then we will go down to the house and meet them,' Cephas said, and started walking down the mountain.

'I do not think that is possible,' Andros replied.

'Why not?' his brother asked.

Andros grinned. 'They would not all fit in the house.'

Cephas stopped and stared at his brother. 'How many?' he asked.

Andros swept an arm in front of himself as they walked round a large rock. 'See for yourself.'

Cephas's eyebrows climbed to his scalp. On a level section of the mountainside so many people had gathered that he could not begin to count them. Men and women, rich and poor, their conversations created a buzz like a hive of giant bees. From group to group, one word was on everyone's lips: 'Yeshua'.

'I've heard he healed a leper.'

'I saw him touch a lame man and he can now walk.'

'My child was deaf and now he can hear.'

'I was blind. Yeshua touched me, and now I can *see*.'

When they saw the Teacher, a cry went up and the crowd surged towards them. Without thinking, Cephas stepped in front of Yeshua lest he be crushed.

'Yeshua, please touch my mother,' one young man pleaded while holding an older woman upright. 'She is sick.'

'Yeshua, my child has uncontrollable seizures,' said a woman, carrying an infant. 'Please touch him.'

'Yeshua, I want to hear more about the kingdom of YHWH,' a man said. 'Is it truly coming soon?' He looked around and lowered his voice, 'Will the Romans truly be overthrown?'

'Stay back, don't crush the Teacher,' Cephas said.

'Cephas, Andros,' Yeshua said, 'tell everyone to sit down and then bring those who are sick to me.' He walked over to a rocky ledge and sat down.

Over the next hour, the disciples brought all those who were sick to Yeshua. He would listen to them, ask a few questions, and then, placing a hand on their head, pray for them. Without fail, each person was healed. When the last person went away rejoicing and thanking YHWH for sending the Messiah, Yeshua turned to face the crowd that remained.

'You want to know about YHWH's kingdom?' he asked.

Across the multitude, heads nodded.

'How can we be part of this kingdom?' one man asked. 'The Pharisees and Sadducees – all the temple leaders – tell us that we have to keep all the Law given to Moses. That is not easy to do. What do we have to do to be acceptable in this new kingdom?'

As Yeshua looked over the crowd, his face softened. 'Being acceptable to YHWH is not a matter of *what you do*,' he said. 'It is a matter of *what is in your heart and what makes you happy.*

'Happy are you who consciously depend on YHWH, knowing that men and women do not have the ability in themselves to please Him. The kingdom belongs to people like them.

'Happy are you who recognize what your needs are and present them to the only One who truly can help. These people will receive help and comfort.'

Yochanan nudged Cephas with his elbow and then nodded his head. At the back of the crowd stood a group of Pharisees. From the way they pulled their richly ornamented robes around themselves, it was obvious they were not pleased with Yeshua's teaching.

'Happy are those who are humble and gentle and understand who they are in this world,' the Teacher continued. 'These people will inherit the earth.

'Happy are those who have a deep desire to do what is right in the eyes of YHWH. This desire will be satisfied.

'Happy are those who show mercy to others. These people will receive mercy themselves.

'Happy are those who repent from their sinful ways and accept forgiveness from YHWH. They will see the Almighty.

'Happy are those who desire to be YHWH's instrument of peace in the world. These people will be known as His children.'

Cephas turned when Yeshua paused. Strangely, the Teacher looked sad for a moment before continuing.

'Happy are those who pursue YHWH and His right-eousness, even if it means they will be persecuted. These people will inherit YHWH's kingdom.

'Happy are those people who are insulted, persecuted and lied about because of me.' Yeshua nodded when several people gasped at this statement. 'Truly,' he said. 'Be glad when this happens, because your reward in heaven will be great. For this same thing happened to the prophets of old.

'Those of YHWH's kingdom are like the salt for the whole earth. Like salt, they help to flavour and preserve the world around them. However, if the salt loses its saltiness, it has no value and needs to be thrown away.'

At that moment, the sunlight shifted, hitting the mountainside. The Teacher noticed many sitting around his feet lifting hands to shield their eyes from its brilliance.

'Those of YHWH's kingdom are the light of the world,' he said. 'A city set on a hill cannot be hidden. You don't light a lamp and then put it under a bowl. No, you put the lamp on a stand, so that it gives light to the whole house. Just like this, those of YHWH's kingdom, let your light shine so that people may see your righteous behaviour and praise *your Father* in heaven.'

'Teacher, what about the Law YHWH gave to Moses?' asked Eleazar from Bethany. 'Will we still follow that?'

'Do not think that the coming of YHWH's kingdom means that the Law given to Moses is no longer important. The Law was given to prepare people for the Messiah and it will stand until *all* the prophecies about YHWH's kingdom are fulfilled. And following these laws goes beyond action,' he added, 'for YHWH looks at your heart.'

'What do you mean?' asked Mayrim, Eleazar's sister.

'You have been taught to ask for forgiveness for your sinful acts. But if you are offering a sacrifice for sin and remember that you have offended someone, leave your offering there. Go and ask forgiveness of the person you offended and then you can present your offering.

'Many will tell you it is all right to hate your enemies. However, I tell you that you should love those who hate you and pray for those who persecute you. By this you will be known as children of YHWH.

'When you do something kind, don't tell anyone. Let these acts be done in secret and your heavenly Father will reward you.

'When you pray, don't do it in public, but go to a private place. And don't think you need to pray long prayers, repeating phrases over and over again. Your Father knows what you need before you pray.'

'Teach us how to pray,' said Marta, Eleazar's other sister.

Yeshua glanced at Cephas, before continuing. 'Talk to YHWH like this:

> Our heavenly Father
> You are to be honoured and worshipped.
> May Your kingdom come and what You want
> Be done on earth as it is in heaven.
> Give us enough to eat today,

Forgive us our wrong acts
As we forgive those who harm us.
Guard us from temptation to do wrong
And protect us from the evil one.
And all this is for Your kingdom, Your power, and
Your glory forever. Amen.

'You mentioned "food for today",' Juda said, 'but what about other things? Like clothes or houses?'

'There is no need to worry about food or drink or clothing,' Yeshua said. 'Isn't life more important than these?' He pointed to a flock of birds flying overhead. 'Look at those birds. They don't scatter seed or harvest and store food; yet your heavenly Father provides their food. Don't you realize that you are worth much more than they are? You cannot add even a single hour to your life by worrying.

'Why do you worry about clothes?' Yeshua pointed to a clump of flowers growing nearby. 'Look at those lilies; they do not work or sew. Yet, not even King Solomon in his richest garments looked like one of these flowers. If this is how YHWH clothes wild flowers, which last only a short time, don't you realize He will provide clothing for you too?

'So don't worry about food or drink or clothes. For those who do not believe in YHWH spend their days running after these things, but your heavenly Father knows that you need them. Make His kingdom and His righteousness the first priority of your life and YHWH will provide for all your needs.'

The Teacher stood, indicating that the time of teaching was over. He lifted his hands. The crowd stood and bowed their heads while he prayed a blessing over them. Then everyone turned to walk down the mountain's slope.

The Twelve gathered around Yeshua as they walked down the rocky path.

'Teacher,' Taoma said, 'you make all of this sound wonderful, but it is hard to believe that all we have to do is ask YHWH for something and He will give it to us.'

Yeshua put a hand on his disciple's shoulder. 'Ah, Taoma,' he said, 'you misunderstood me. I did not say that YHWH will give you whatever you *want*; I said He would provide what you *need*.'

They passed a man who was walking with a child.

'Daddy, Daddy,' the child said. 'I'm hungry. May I have some bread?'

The man – who was obviously the child's father – reached into a bag slung across his shoulders and took out a piece of bread to hand to the child.

'Did you think that was unusual for the child to ask his father for food?' Yeshua asked.

'No,' Taoma answered.

'Would a good father give his child a stone in place of bread?'

'No.'

Yeshua pointed to a group of rocks, where a snake's tail was seen slithering away.

'What if the child asks for a fish; would a good father give him a snake?'

'No!' Taoma answered.

'If an earthly father, even though he is not perfect, would give his child the things he needs, don't you think your heavenly Father – who is perfect – would give His children the things He knows they need?'

'Teacher, as you said, earthly fathers and children are not perfect,' Shimon said as they left the mountain and walked towards the village. 'Don't we need to be perfect, so that we get these things from our heavenly Father?'

'Shimon, children do not need to *earn* their father's love; not even the ones who hurt their fathers,' Yeshua said. 'Let me tell you a story.

'There was a wealthy man who had two sons; the older son was a hard worker and obeyed his father, but the younger son was lazy and disobeyed his father.

'One day, the younger son came to his father and demanded his portion of the inheritance *right then*, even though his father was still alive. The father agreed and, estimating the value of his estate, gave the younger son his part.

'Several days later, the younger son packed his things and left. He moved far away – where no one knew him – and soon wasted all his inheritance on wild living. About that time, a famine struck the land and he began to starve. He found a farmer who hired him to care for the pigs; sometimes he was so hungry that he was tempted to eat some of the food he was giving to the animals.

'After a while, the young man came to his senses. "My father is a wealthy man," he said, "and he feeds the men who work for him. I will go home and tell him that I do not consider myself worthy of being his son and beg him to hire me. At least I won't starve."

'The young man returned home. When he turned down the path to his home, his father – who had watched every day for him – saw him coming. He ran to his son and threw his arms around him, crying.

'"Father," the young man said, "I am not worthy to be considered your son . . ."

'The father interrupted him, calling to his servants to bring a clean robe and sandals for his son and to prepare a huge banquet.

'When the older son returned from working in the fields, he heard the sound of the celebration and asked a servant about it. When he heard that his younger brother had returned, he refused to go inside. His father came out and begged him to come to the party.

'"No," he said. "I have worked all these years and never asked for anything from you. And now this *son of yours* – who wasted all the money you gave him on wild living – has returned and *you want to celebrate?*"

'"Son," his father said, "you are dear to me and everything I have is yours. But we had to celebrate this happy moment. For *your brother* – who was as good as dead – has come back to life. He was lost and now he is found."'

* * *

The disciples walked through the market place, looking at the wares the merchants were selling. Yeshua selected some fruit and nuts and honey.

'Juda, please pay this merchant,' he said, handing the basket of food to Cephas. 'Do you think Ruth can make those sweet cakes that my mother made?'

Cephas grinned. 'I'm sure she can.'

Yeshua turned round and found a spot in the shade near the synagogue. He leaned up against the building and watched the people going by.

Standing in front the synagogue several priests were speaking with a man who was dressed in rich clothing. A man dressed in rags had paused a few steps away – obviously waiting to speak to one of the priests.

After a moment, a priest noticed the poor man and walked over to him. 'What do you want?' he asked.

'Sir, may I speak in private with you?'

The priest looked at him with open disdain.

'Can't you see that we are busy with this *gentleman* and do not have time to speak with you now. Go away.'

'Let me tell you a story,' Yeshua said to the Twelve. 'Two men went to the temple to pray. One was a Pharisee and the other a dishonest tax collector.' He noticed Levi look down and shuffle his feet. 'Levi, I assure you that you will like this story.'

'The Pharisee was quite proud; he stood in the middle of the temple and prayed out loud, "YHWH, I thank You that

I am not a sinner *like that tax collector*. I don't cheat anyone *like he does*, I don't do anything wrong. I fast and pray twice a week and give one tenth of my earnings to the temple."

'The tax collector found a corner to pray. He did not even look towards heaven, but bowed his head in sorrow. "YHWH, I have sinned," he whispered. 'Please forgive me."

'Believe me, it was this sinner – and not the Pharisee – who pleased YHWH. Those who are proud will be humbled and those who are humbled will be honoured.'

Several of the Twelve smiled to hear a Pharisee cast in a bad light, while Cephas, Yochanan and Yaakov laughed aloud.

One of the priests who had overheard Yeshua's story walked towards them, bristling with offence. He barely nodded his head to Yeshua. 'Greetings, Teacher,' he said and pointedly ignored the disciples.

'Teacher,' he said, 'I have heard that you speak of a *never-ending life* in YHWH's kingdom. Tell me, what must I do to please YHWH and get this life?

Yeshua looked at the man. 'What does the Law of Moses say about pleasing YHWH?'

The man puffed up his chest. 'It says,' he responded in a booming voice that drew a small crowd, including the other priests, '"You must love YHWH with everything that is inside you – heart, soul and mind."' After a pause – as if an afterthought – he added, 'Oh yes, and "Love your neighbour as much as you love yourself."'

Yeshua nodded. 'You are correct,' he said. 'Do this and you will receive the life you desire.'

The priest glanced around at the gathered crowd and asked, 'Who is *my neighbour?*'

Yeshua stared at the man silently for a moment; the priest shifted under the Teacher's penetrating glance.

'Let me tell you a story,' he said softly. The people around him moved closer to listen. 'A man was travelling from Jerusalem to Jericho, when he was attacked by robbers. They beat him, took his money – and most of his clothes – and left him dying on the roadside.

'In a little while, a priest came by. He saw the man but – because he didn't want to violate the Law of Moses by touching someone who might already be dead – he moved to the far side of the road and went on.

'Not long after that, someone who helped in the temple also walked by. Like the priest, he kept as far away from the man as he could and continued walking down the road.

'Soon after him, a Samaritan came down the road . . .'

A murmur ran through the crowd, many of them commenting on the 'filthy Samaritan dogs'.

'This Samaritan got off his donkey and knelt down by the man. Then he got some water and bathed the man's wounds and wrapped them with clean cloths. He lifted the man onto his own donkey, took him to a nearby inn and paid for a room where he could better care for the man.

'The next morning, the Samaritan gave the innkeeper some money, with instructions to care for this man. "If his care costs more than this," he said, "I will pay the difference when I come here the next time." '

Yeshua looked at the priest who had asked the question. 'Now, which man do you think was a *neighbour* to the man who was attacked?'

The priest looked at the crowd and glanced at the other priests. Then he looked back at Yeshua. 'The one who was kind to him,' he whispered.

The Teacher nodded, 'Yes. Now you do the same. For the whole Law of Moses and all its teachings is summed up in this statement, "Do to others what you wish they would do for you." '

10

The Miracles

Even though the setting sun cast hues of orange and gold across the Sea of Galilee, a large crowd were still gathered on the beach to hear Yeshua teach. As the deepening sky took an edge off the razor-sharp heat, a large black snake slithered from the protection of several rocks, followed by a rat.

'Look at *Him*,' the snake sneered. 'Teaching those wretched *humans*. As if they will even remember – much less care about – what He says.'

'Well, Lucifer, the crowd do seem to be paying attention,' the rat observed. Then, squealing, it jumped back as the snake lunged at him.

'Don't *ever* correct me again, Wormwood!' the snake hissed at the cringing rat.

'I'm sorry, Master,' Wormwood said. 'But, shouldn't we pay attention to how those humans respond to Him?'

The snake turned its slitted eyes towards the crowd. 'Hmmmm,' it mused, 'perhaps you are right. They do seem to be listening attentively. Maybe we should do something.'

'What can we do to Him?' the rat asked, scratching his ear. 'After all, He is—'

'Shhh . . .' The snake silenced his companion. 'The "teaching" is ending. Let's listen; maybe we can think of something.'

* * *

The Teacher's hands were raised over the crowd in a final blessing. As he turned, he closed his eyes and took a deep breath.

'Yeshua,' Andros asked, 'are you all right?'

Yeshua nodded. 'I'm fine,' he responded. 'Just a little tired.'

'It's no wonder you're tired,' Cephas said. 'You've been teaching this crowd since early this morning. You need to rest.'

The Teacher paused, tilting his head as if he were listening to . . . *someone*. 'Yochanan, Yaakov, aren't those your father's boats over there?' he asked, pointing to several vessels that had been pulled onto the beach and secured with a rope tied around a large rock.

'Yes, they are,' Yochanan said.

'Do you think my Uncle Zebedee would mind if we used one?' Yeshua asked. 'We must go to the other side of the Sea of Galilee and this would be easier than walking.'

'I'm sure Father would not mind at all if we used one of the boats,' Yochanan said. 'Let me run and ask him.'

A little while later, he returned to say that Zebedee was most happy to let his sons and his nephew use a boat. Yochanan climbed in and turned to help Yeshua into the boat. The other disciples followed.

The fishing vessel was large and even after all the Twelve had climbed aboard there would have been room for a few more. Yaakov untied the rope and jumped on board; he stowed the rope at the stern of the boat.

'Yeshua,' he said, 'you don't need to help sail the boat. There is a small compartment back here where you can lie down and rest. We even have a pillow you can place under your head.'

'Thank you, Cousin,' Yeshua said. 'I am weary.' Climbing into the small resting place, the Teacher lay down.

A few minutes later, Yaakov nudged Yochanan and nodded his head in the direction of the stern; their cousin was fast asleep. They smiled at each other.

The disciples who were fisherman manned the boat, while those who had come from different occupations spent the time talking or trying to ease stomachs made seasick from the movement of the vessel.

Cephas looked up at the clouds gathering in the darkening sky and tried to determine how long it would take them to reach the distant shore. From the mountains came thunder that rattled through the heavens. A bolt of lightning shot through the black clouds and thunder rumbled like an avalanche across the sky. The gale grew until a screaming wind from the east was whipping huge waves onto the deck. The ship began to roll on the water as if it would sink in the deluge.

Cephas grabbed some coiled ropes and tossed them to the other disciples. 'Tie yourself to the boat,' he instructed.

'Is it common for storms to grow this fierce?' Levi asked worriedly, wrapping the rope around his waist.

'Well, storms *are* common on the Sea of Galilee,' Cephas yelled over the howling wind. 'But I don't remember one like this.'

The fishermen tried to sail the vessel. None of the Twelve, whether experienced sailors or not, was able to tolerate the jerking of the boat as it was tossed by waves like small mountains. It rolled back and forth, lifted into the air by the high waves and then dumped into the dark chasms that fell away. Whatever food or drink was in their stomachs was emptied over the side.

After one monstrous wave nearly capsized the boat, Cephas yelled, 'Andros, count to make certain we are all here. I'll check on Yeshua.'

Cephas untied his rope and pulled himself hand over hand along the edge of the boat – losing his footing when the waves tilted the vessel – to the stern. Grabbing the door to the small compartment, he opened it.

There he saw Yeshua totally at rest.

Reaching down, Cephas grabbed the Teacher's shoulder and shook him. 'Yeshua! Teacher,' he cried. 'Wake up. Don't you care if we all drown?'

Yeshua opened his eyes as lightning illuminated Cephas's wide-eyed fear and the fury of the storm raging around them. Yeshua pulled himself up. Lightning sizzled across the sky – mere inches from the single mast – revealing the terrified faces of the disciples.

Reaching towards the sky, Yeshua yelled, 'You have no power over me or my Father's creation! Stop this now! PEACE, BE STILL.'

Instantly, as if he had cast out a demon, the storm stopped. It didn't lessen, it didn't gradually slow down; it stopped suddenly and without question.

Cephas and the others gasped. A gentle breeze blew across the water's surface and the moonlight shone through a clear sky.

'Why were you afraid?' Yeshua asked his disciples. 'I told you we were going to the other side of the sea. Do you have so little faith?' Turning round, he crawled back into the compartment at the stern and closed the door.

For several moments, no one said anything . . .

'Cephas,' Andros stuttered in fear, 'Yeshua just told the storm to stop and it *obeyed* him!'

'Who is *he* that he can do this?' Netanel asked.

Levi whispered aloud what each man was thinking as the growing revelation came to his lips. 'Only *YHWH* can command the wind and the waves.' He looked around at the peaceful night and then at the compartment in the stern of the boat. 'Only YHWH.'

The sea remained peaceful. The Twelve kept as silent as the night as they sailed the boat to the distant shore. After securing the vessel with the rope wrapped around a large boulder, they removed their wet tunics and robes and spread them over the rocks. Then they stretched out on the beach.

'I'm not sleeping in that boat,' Levi muttered – and fell into an exhausted sleep.

'Cephas . . .' Yeshua nudged the sleeping disciple with his foot. 'Wake up.'

Cephas rolled over and rubbed the sand off his face. He looked up to see Yeshua standing over him, grinning.

'Good morning, Cephas. Did you rest well?' the Teacher asked.

'Yes, I did,' Cephas blustered as he pulled on his robe.

'I'm hungry,' Yeshua said. 'And I'm sure you are as well. Yochanan, Juda, go into the village and buy us something to eat.'

While the two disciples were gone, the others finished dressing and then cleaned up the fishing boat. Less than an hour had passed when Juda and Yochanan came running back without any food.

'Yeshua!' Yochanan ran to grab his cousin's arm. 'We just heard the news.'

The Twelve gathered around them. 'What news?' Cephas asked.

'Our cousin, the Baptizer,' Yochanan began and then broke down crying.

'What is it?' Andros said. 'What happened? Juda?'

Juda looked at Yochanan and then at Yeshua and finally at the others. 'We were in the market place when we over-heard some people talking,' he said. 'The Baptizer is dead.'

'What?' A horrified gasp rippled through the men.

'Dead?' Taoma asked. 'How?'

Juda told them that King Herod had given a party to celebrate the day of his birth and had asked his step-daughter, Salome, to dance for the guests. Herod was so pleased that he announced he would give the girl whatever she wanted, even if it was half of his kingdom.

'Herod does not have the authority to give away any of his kingdom,' Shimon said. 'He rules it for Rome.'

'Well, he promised it to her,' Juda said. 'Salome asked her mother what she should ask for and Herodias said . . .' he choked up, 'the *head* of Yochanan the Baptizer on a silver platter.'

'What?' the men gasped again in shocked disbelief.

'And Herod gave it to her?' Thaddai asked.

Juda nodded. 'Herod gave it to her,' he whispered.

Yeshua, tears streaming into his beard, walked over to Yochanan and wrapped his arms around his weeping cousin. Yaakov stumbled over and embraced his brother and cousin. The others stood quietly while their three friends grieved the loss of one many considered to be as great as the prophet Elijah.

After several minutes, Cephas walked up to Yeshua. 'Come, Teacher, I know of a solitary place nearby where you and Yochanan and Yaakov can be private in your grief.'

'Thank you, Cephas,' Yeshua said. 'You are a good friend.'

11

People Healed, People Fed

It took an hour to reach the secluded place. Trees provided relief from the burning sunlight and grass was soft under the men's feet. Yeshua, Yochanan and Yaakov sat down in the shade and spoke quietly to each other, occasionally wiping away tears.

The others moved a short distance away, allowing their friends privacy. When the other men asked, Juda explained that he and Yochanan had not purchased any food. 'We heard about the Baptizer before we bought anything,' he said, 'and we returned immediately.'

Cephas put his hand on Juda's shoulder. 'You did the right thing,' he said. 'We can go for food in a while.'

The rest of the disciples sat down; they spoke quietly about their memories of the Baptizer. After a while, Yeshua, Yochanan and Yaakov returned to join this conversation.

'I cannot believe he is gone,' Yaakov said, wiping his eyes.

'If he was a prophet like so many people thought,' Taoma said, 'why wouldn't YHWH protect him?'

'Taoma, you remember the ancient stories from our history,' Andros said. 'Our forefathers did not live a life without problems. Joseph was sold into slavery, lied about and thrown into prison. Daniel was thrown into the den of lions.'

'Yes, but in each of those stories, the prophet was saved from death,' Taoma replied. 'Why not the Baptizer?'

'Oh no,' Cephas said before anyone had time to reply. He pointed beyond the shady grove. 'Look.'

Turning, the disciples saw a multitude of people approaching. Here and there were people with broken arms, others were walking with the aid of crutches and some were dragging their friends on stretchers.

When they saw Yeshua, one man cried out, 'There he is! There's the Teacher!' The crowd surged towards the disciples.

'Can they not leave us alone for a moment?' Cephas growled as he stood.

'Don't worry, Teacher, I'll send them away.'

Yeshua placed a hand on Cephas's forearm. 'No,' he said quietly. 'Let me speak to them.'

He stood and walked to the crowd. After quietly greeting them, he turned to a young woman who held a baby.

'He is blind,' the young mother said. 'He could see when he was born, but a fever robbed him of his sight. The doctors can do nothing for him.'

Taking the baby in his arms, Yeshua closed his eyes and prayed over him. Then he kissed the infant's forehead and handed him back to his mother. As the Teacher turned to an elderly man, the mother waved a hand in front of her baby.

'He can see!' she cried out. 'Praise be to YHWH! My son is healed.'

For the next few hours, Yeshua walked through the multitude, praying for those who were sick, or crippled, or deaf or blind: each person was healed. At last, he walked to where his disciples were, took a water skin from Philippos and drank deeply. Then he looked back at the crowd, who were exclaiming over the miracles they had just witnessed.

'We should feed these people,' the Teacher said. 'Where can we buy some bread?'

Philippos stared at him in amazement; what could Yeshua mean?

'Teacher,' he said incredulously, 'even if we had eight months' wages, that wouldn't be enough to buy bread for each one of these people to have just one bite.'

'Go, ask among the people,' Yeshua said, 'and see whether anyone has some food.'

The disciples looked at each other. After a moment, Cephas shrugged his shoulders and nodded his head in the direction of the crowd. The Twelve turned and began to walk among the people.

Some time later, Andros returned with a boy at his side. 'Teacher, this boy has some food.'

Yeshua smiled at the lad. 'Hello,' he said. 'What is your name?'

'Eli,' the boy replied.

'Eli, Andros tells me that you wish to share your food,' Yeshua smiled.

'I do, Teacher,' Eli handed a bag to Yeshua. 'Before I left home this morning, my mother gave me five small barley loaves and two fish for my lunch. My mother and father always taught me to share whatever I had with those who had nothing. It's not much, but I would like to share.'

Yeshua ruffled Eli's curly hair. 'Thank you, Eli; I will remember your generosity.'

Yeshua called his disciples to him. 'Tell the people to sit down in groups.'

It took a while to carry out the Teacher's request. 'I've been counting, Thaddai said when they returned, 'and there are about five thousand men, not to mention the women and children.'

Yeshua took Eli's lunch and lifted it towards the sky. 'Father, You always provide for those who love You. Thank You for sending Eli to bless so many with his generous gift.'

Lowering his hands, he handed the bag back to the boy. 'Would you please hold the bag?'

Then he took a barley loaf and tore it in half; he handed the two halves to Cephas. 'Give these out and then come back.' Breaking one of the fish into pieces, he handed them to Andros. 'Follow your brother and give these out as well.'

Yeshua repeated this action with Yochanan and Yaakov, and he handed a broken barley loaf to Netanel.

When Philippos stepped forward, the disciple gasped; the Teacher held two more pieces of fish. He glanced at the bag in Eli's hands; it was bulging with fish and bread. 'T-teacher,' he stammered, 'where did you get . . .' But the rest of his shocked words faded.

Yeshua looked at his disciple and smiled as he handed him the fish.

Even with the Twelve it took a long time for everyone to get something to eat. After a while, the people began refusing the disciples' offer of more food, stating that they were full to bursting.

'Cephas, Andros, you and the rest of the Twelve find some baskets,' Yeshua said. 'Gather the pieces of fish and bread that are left. We do not want to waste anything.'

The disciples looked at each other. 'Food left over?' Taoma commented.

'You heard him,' Cephas said. 'Find some baskets. Gather the food.' By the time the sun was setting, the Twelve stood around Yeshua, with the leftover food.

'How many baskets of food were left?' a man in the crowd asked.

'Twelve,' Cephas answered.

A roar went up from the multitude.

'Yeshua fed us with bread and fish, just like the manna and quail YHWH provided in the wilderness,' one man said.

'The bread never stopped, just like the prophet, Elijah, and the widow's oil and flour,' said a woman.

'Surely, the *Messiah* would provide all our needs,' someone else cried out.

'He has come!' the cry was repeated through the crowd. 'The Messiah has come!'

12

The Deaf-Mute

'Teacher, I think I have prayed more since I met you than I did in all the rest of my life,' Cephas said, as he, Yaakov, Yochanan and Yeshua stepped off the slopes of Mount Hermon. 'But I *still* can't pray for very long. I just don't know what to pray about.'

Yeshua put an arm around the disciple's shoulder. 'Cephas, when you were a child, how did you know what your father wanted you to do?'

Cephas shrugged. 'I asked him.'

Yeshua smiled. 'That is what I am doing when I pray,' he said. 'I need to know what YHWH wants me to do every day. Sometimes I need to get away by myself for a longer time of prayer. Other times, like today, I like to have some friends to pray with me.'

'We are to meet the rest of the Twelve in Caesarea Philippi, is that right?' Yochanan asked.

Yeshua nodded. 'Yes it is.'

'I hope they've bought some food,' Cephas laughed, rubbing his stomach. 'I'm hungry.'

'What is that?' Yaakov asked, pointing.

A large crowd had gathered down the road that led from the mountain towards the town of Caesarea Philippi. Many were yelling; some shook fists at those on the opposite side of the crowd. As Yeshua and the three men got closer, they could see Andros, Levi and the rest of the disciples standing in the centre of the angry mob.

A man on the outer edge of the crowd looked round and saw Yeshua. 'Look!' he pointed. 'It's the Teacher!' He – along with others from the crowd – ran towards Yeshua.

'You are here at last,' the man said. 'You can settle the matter.'

The crowd opened up to let Yeshua walk to their midst. He nodded to his disciples. 'What is all the arguing about?'

'Teacher,' a man stepped up to Yeshua and bowed, 'my name is Ophir. I brought my son, Kenan, for you to heal him. He is possessed by a demon that robbed him of his voice and hearing.' Ophir wrung his hands in despair. 'That isn't all. Sometimes this evil spirit seizes Kenan and throws him to the ground, causing him to writhe in horrible convulsions and foam at the mouth. I am afraid that one day, the demon will kill my son.

'I was in the marketplace today when I heard someone say you and your disciples were here. I tried to find you, but your disciples told me that you were not with them, so I asked if they could help my son.'

'We tried to cast the demon out, Teacher,' Levi said. 'But we couldn't do it.'

'That's when these teachers of the Law approached us,' Shimon the Zealot flung a hand towards three men dressed in fine robes standing opposite them. 'They told us we did not have the *right* to help this boy and all but accused us of practising witchcraft.'

The crowd erupted into angry voices. One of the teachers of the Law lifted his hands in protest; the noise subsided. He turned to Yeshua. 'I am Tobias ben Joktan, a teacher of the Law of Moses and elder of the synagogue. You are Yeshua, the teacher from *Nazareth*?' His tone implied what he thought of the little town.

Yeshua nodded.

'We have heard the reports of you,' the teacher of the Law said. 'Some claim that you have . . . *great powers*.' Tobias gestured to the men with him. 'As elders in this city and teachers of the Law of YHWH, it is our responsibility to examine such reports. The news of men trying to cast out demons spread like a fire through a field of grain. We came to witness this great act and to question the *source* of their – and your – authority to command demons.' The man smirked. 'Of course, since they were *unable* to help poor Kenan . . .' he spread his hands and shrugged, 'perhaps the reports about you were . . . *exaggerated*?'

Shimon raised a fist. 'Are you trying to say that we . . .'

'Stop,' Yeshua said. He looked at the teacher of the Law and his companions; they crossed their arms, smiling smugly. 'Faithless.'

Tobias ben Joktan's jaw dropped. 'W-w-what?' he spluttered, his face growing red. 'Are you–?'

Yeshua interrupted the teacher of the Law. He turned in a circle, taking in the crowd as well as his disciples. 'You are all faithless! How long must I be with you before you believe who I am?' He looked at Ophir, who stood wringing his hands. 'Bring your son to me.'

Ophir glanced at the teachers of the Law and then back at Yeshua. He nodded. 'I'll fetch him right now.'

Tobias watched Ophir running towards the town and then turned back to Yeshua. 'What do you think you are going to do?' he asked.

Yeshua looked at him for a moment and closed his eyes.

'Well?' Tobias snapped.

When Yeshua did not answer – or even open his eyes – the teacher of the Law looked at the disciples. 'What is he doing?' he asked. 'Why doesn't he answer me?'

Cephas glanced at Yeshua and then at Tobias; he smiled. 'He's praying.'

Tobias frowned, his eyebrows lowered in a point over his prominent nose. 'Praying?' He turned to look at his companions. 'He's praying?' They shrugged and shook their heads. Tobias turned back to face Yeshua. 'Now see here, I am not accustomed to being treated this way. I insist that you answer me.'

Yeshua did not move, but continued praying.

'Look! There's Ophir. He's got Kenan,' someone in the crowd said. 'Give him room. Give him room!'

Ophir walked up to Yeshua, holding the hand of a young boy. 'Teacher, this is my son, Kenan,' he said.

The boy – who appeared to be about ten – had been looking around curiously at the crowd. When he turned and saw Yeshua, he hissed and pulled back, jerking out of his father's grasp. The boy fell to the ground as if thrown by an invisible hand; his head rebounded against the packed earth. His body jerked in a writhing convulsion; he screamed and snarled and gnashed his teeth, foaming at the mouth.

Gasps shot through the crowd as people stepped away from the thrashing boy.

'How long has this been happening?' Yeshua asked.

'Since he was very small,' Ophir said, kneeling by his son. He tried to grasp Kenan's hands, yet avoid his snapping jaws. 'At first, the demon took away his hearing and then his voice. Then came the writhing spells.' He turned to look at Yeshua. 'Now the evil spirit causes him to fall into the fire or into water, trying to kill him.'

Ophir jumped up and lifted his hand, bloody from Kenan's teeth. He untied the cloth belt around his waist and wrapped his hand to stop the bleeding. 'Please, sir. Have mercy. If you can do something, please help us.'

'If?' Yeshua asked. 'What do you mean, "If I can?" With YHWH, anything is possible for those who believe.'

Ophir lifted his hands – blood soaking through the cloth belt. 'I do believe,' he sobbed. 'I do . . . I try . . . I mean, please help me to believe. Help me not to doubt.'

Yeshua nodded and then pointed at Kenan still writhing on the ground. 'Demon, listen to me!' he said. 'I command you to come out of this boy!'

The boy thrashed wildly, arms and legs rigid; his screams grew louder and higher and then suddenly stopped.

First one and then another of the crowd took hesitant steps towards the boy lying motionless on the ground.

'He's healed,' a woman said in awe.

'He's not healed,' said another, 'he's dead.'

Yeshua stooped and took Kenan's hand. The boy's eyes moved slowly under closed lids and, after a moment, opened. He stared into Yeshua's face and then smiled. The Teacher stood and helped Kenan up.

The boy looked around as if unsure where he was or who the people were. When he saw his father, still holding his bloodied hand, he stepped towards him. He opened his mouth and licked his lips.

'P-p-pa . . .' Kenan looked at Yeshua, who nodded encouragement, and then back at his father. 'Papa?' he whispered?

Ophir gasped, his eyes widened. He reached out and hesitantly touched his son's head, gazing into the boy's eyes. 'Kenan.'

'Papa.' Kenan smiled.

Ophir grasped his son's shoulder and pulled him to his chest. 'Kenan! Praise YHWH!' He looked over his son's head at Yeshua. 'Thank you!' He took a shuddering breath. 'Thank you! Please, I would be most honoured if you and your disciples would come to my house for supper.'

Yeshua nodded. 'We would be most honoured to accept your kind invitation.'

'Come, Kenan,' Ophir laughed, 'we must hurry home and prepare for our guests. It is a day to celebrate YHWH's goodness!'

Ophir and his son hurried down the road, followed by a crowd of people who were laughing and shouting.

All the teachers of the Law stared open-mouthed as the crowd left and then turned to look at Yeshua. Tobias ben Joktan opened his mouth to say something to the Teacher and then shook his head. He straightened his robes and, gesturing to his companions, turned to stride down the dirt road.

Yeshua closed his eyes. 'Thank you, Father,' he whispered.

'Teacher?'

Yeshua opened his eyes and looked at Levi. The disciple shifted from one foot to another.

'Why?' Levi looked at Shimon and the other disciples. 'We tried,' he said, 'but we couldn't cast out the demon. Why?'

Yeshua began walking down the road towards Caesarea Philippi and his disciples fell in alongside him. 'Faith,' he said.

'Faith?' Levi asked.

'Levi,' Yeshua asked, 'did your father love you?'

'Love me?' the disciple's brow furrowed, 'Yes, he loved me.'

'If your father asked you to do something,' Yeshua said, 'would he not have provided you with the tools necessary to do that task?'

Levi nodded, 'Yes, he would.'

'That was because of the love he had for you; you had faith in that love, did you not?'

Levi nodded again.

'It's the same with YHWH, your heavenly Father. If you have faith in him – if you believe and trust in the love he has for you – even if the faith is only the size of a tiny mustard seed, you can tell that mountain,' Yeshua pointed to a nearby mountain, ' "Move from here . . ." ' he swung his arm to point to the opposite side, ' "to there," and it *will move*.

'With that kind of faith,' Yeshua said, *'nothing* YHWH tells you to do will be impossible.'

13

The Siblings

Marta surged through the room, dusting and straightening anything in her path. Her robe had smudges of dirt and splatters of food, and several wisps of damp hair had escaped her head cloth. She turned at the sound of approaching footsteps and sighed in frustration when her younger sister, Mayrim, walked in, carrying a basket filled with wild flowers. The cleanliness of Mayrim's robe – and her head cloth neatly covering her hair – irritated Marta.

'Have you been gathering flowers all morning?' she asked.

Mayrim arched an eyebrow at the critical tone in her sister's voice. 'Yes, I have,' she said. 'The Teacher is coming today and I thought the flowers would make the house smell lovely.'

Marta snapped. 'I have been cooking and cleaning the house – by myself – since dawn in preparation for the Teacher's visit.'

Mayrim set the basket down and crossed her arms. 'Are you suggesting that *you* are the only one who cares about the Teacher's visit?'

Marta folded her arms. 'Well, I guess you might think that,' she said, 'since *I* am the only one who has *done anything useful* to prepare for his visit.'

'Please don't argue,' their brother Eleazar asked as he entered the room. 'We don't have time. Yeshua and the Twelve will be here soon.' He handed a wrapped package to Marta. 'Here is the fish you wanted.'

'Fish?' Mayrim asked. 'We already have lamb for the meal. Why do you want fish as well?'

Marta sniffed the fish to make sure it was fresh. 'I want to make the meal special for the Teacher,' she said.

'Yeshua doesn't care about food,' Mayrim said. 'Cephas told me that he usually eats a simple meal.'

'That's probably because Yeshua usually stays with people who cannot afford more,' Marta replied. 'We can afford it and it would appear tight-fisted to serve him bread and cheese when we can have lamb and fish.' She turned and carried the fish out of the room.

When Mayrim started to follow her sister, Eleazar laid a hand on her arm. 'Let her go, Mayrim,' he said. 'You know how Marta gets when we have guests. She has got to have the best of everything.'

Mayrim sighed and nodded. 'You're right, Eleazar,' she said. 'I shouldn't have let her anger me, but to imply that I do not care about the Teacher's visit . . .'

'I know,' her brother replied. 'I hope one day she will learn that just because *she* thinks something is important that doesn't make it so.'

'I do too,' Mayrim agreed. 'Meanwhile I will apologize and offer to help with the meal. I know Yeshua likes date and honey cakes; maybe I have time to make some before he and the Twelve arrive.'

No sooner had the sisters begun to cook than their house filled with guests. Yeshua and the disciples sat inside whilst those who followed waited outside.

'Marta, Mayrim, the meal is delicious,' Yeshua said, as he reached for a piece of flatbread. He grinned at his host. 'Eleazar, you are a dear friend, but there are other reasons I love coming here.'

'Thank you, Teacher,' Mayrim said, 'but Marta made most of the meal.'

'Thank you, Teacher,' Marta said and paused. 'Mayrim brought in flowers . . . and made some date and honey cakes.'

'Date and honey cakes are one of my favourites,' Yeshua laughed.

'Teacher,' Eleazar said, 'would you please tell the story of the two builders? I cannot remember it.'

'When someone listens to my teachings and obeys me, that person is like the man who built a house on a strong foundation of rock. When the floodwaters rose, the house stood firm, because it was built upon the rock. But those who listen to my words and do not obey are like the man who built a house on sand. When the floods came, his house collapsed.'

'Mayrim,' Marta whispered, 'Mayrim.' The younger sister stood transfixed, listening to Yeshua. Marta nudged her. '*Mayrim*!' she hissed.

'Huh?' Mayrim looked at her sister, who nodded towards the inner door. 'Oh, I'm sorry,' she said, following Marta.

The siblings' house had one large room at the front and another at the back. The front room was used to entertain guests and back room was divided into sleeping quarters. The walls were covered with smooth clay and the floors – unlike the homes of poorer people – were tile, although of simple design. In the outside courtyard, hung an awning to provide shade for a low table and several benches. Stairs along the side of the house led to the roof, where Marta, Mayrim and Eleazar – along with their guests – would sit to enjoy the cool evening breezes.

Marta was already in the far corner of the courtyard where a table – covered in food and dishes – stood near a clay oven. She basted the lamb roasting on a spit over the fire and then turned to the table to place several sprigs of rosemary on top of the baked fish.

'Here,' she handed the platter to Mayrim, 'take this in to our guests. The lamb is nearly ready and I cannot leave it or it will burn.' As Mayrim turned away, carrying the platter, Marta called after her, 'And hurry back.'

While Marta waited for the lamb to finish roasting, she mixed together mint and spices into a dipping sauce that was known throughout the area of Bethany. She poured it into one of her good crockery bowls. She lifted the lamb from the spit and carefully transferred it to a large serving platter. Marta placed the bowl of mint sauce on the platter and then scattered several mint leaves around the lamb to enhance its appearance. 'It looks perfect,' she said with a smile as she lifted the platter to carry it to their guests. 'The Teacher will *love* this.'

Marta hummed to herself as she imagined the compliments she would receive for this meal. From the flatbread and crumbly white cheese, the freshest olives she could find in the market, the fish and now the lamb, it was all perfect. The meal would finish with Mayrim's date and honey cakes and a bowl of almonds.

She walked across the courtyard, looked through the doorway and . . . gasped.

The platter with the fish was on the table, but Mayrim was not serving their guests. She was sitting on the floor next to Yeshua, listening to him talk.

'Mayrim!'

Everyone – including Yeshua – turned to look at her.

Marta had not meant to screech, but finding Mayrim sitting – and doing *nothing* – had surprised her. She felt her cheeks grow hot with embarrassment and she spoke the first thing that came to her mind. 'Teacher, don't you care that Mayrim has left me to do all the work by myself? Tell her to come and help me.'

Everyone's eyes swivelled towards Mayrim and then Yeshua. He looked at the young woman sitting at his feet who stared at the floor, her cheeks tinged with spots of colour. He then looked back at Marta, who lifted her nose and sniffed in condescension.

'Marta, Marta,' he said, shaking his head slightly. 'You are worried about things that have no real value and tomorrow will be gone. The thing that Mayrim chose – to listen to lessons about YHWH – has eternal value. *That* can never be taken from her.

14

Raised from the Dead!

'Eleazar, do you feel all right?' Marta asked.

Eleazar stood at the door to the courtyard. His skin looked pale in the sunlight and he was trembling even though the morning air was warm.

'I do not feel well at all,' her brother replied. 'I hurt all over and the mere thought of food makes me queasy.'

'Go and lie down,' Mayrim said. 'We will bring you some cool mint and barley water to drink.' She watched her brother go back to his bed and turned to her sister. 'Should we send for the physician?'

'Not yet,' Marta said as she crossed the courtyard to prepare the herbal drink. 'Let us watch him.'

Despite several cups of soothing drink, Eleazar continued to grow worse. When he developed a fever, Marta immediately sent for the physician. He gave the sisters several more herbs, with instructions on how to prepare them, and said he would check on their brother the next morning.

By morning, however, Eleazar was delirious with fever and couldn't even keep down the barley water. The physician told the sisters there was nothing more he could do. 'You must prepare yourself for the worst,' he said.

'No!' Mayrim embraced Marta, crying. 'There must be something we can do.'

'But what?' Marta asked. 'The doctor has done everything.'

'Let's send for Yeshua!' Mayrim said. 'Remember how Cephas told us that his mother-in-law had been sick with a fever and she recovered when the Teacher prayed for her.'

'Do you know where the Teacher is?' Marta asked.

'No,' Mayrim said, 'but we can send messengers to all the places we know he visits. Surely one will find Yeshua.'

It took three days for the word of the sickness that gripped Eleazar to reach Yeshua. From town to town the men searched for him. In every place they were sent another league further as people pointed the way. Finding the house where the Teacher was staying, the messenger banged urgently on the door.

'Yeshua, there is a messenger for you,' Ruth, Cephas's wife, said.

A man entered the room. His robe and face was dusty from travelling. After greeting all in the room, he turned to Yeshua. 'Are you Yeshua?' he asked. 'The one they call, *the Teacher*?'

'I am,' Yeshua answered.

'I have a message for you,' he said. When Yeshua nodded, the man stepped closer and began whispering in the Teacher's ear. As he listened to the message Yeshua closed his eyes. After a moment, the messenger straightened, bowed and left.

The Twelve waited. The Twelve recognized Yeshua's closed eyes as a sign he was praying.

'What did the man say?' Cephas asked when Yeshua opened his eyes again.

'The message was from Mayrim and Marta,' he said. 'They said, "Teacher, the one you love is sick."' He looked at his disciples. 'But this sickness will not end in death. It will be used for YHWH's glory and that His Son may receive glory as well.'

'Shall we not go to him?' Cephas asked.

Yeshua smiled. 'This sickness will not end in death,' he repeated.

Two days later, after they had finished the morning meal, Yeshua seemed distracted.

'We need to go back to Judea to the house of Marta and Mayrim.'

'Why?' Taoma asked.

'Eleazar has fallen asleep,' the Teacher said, 'and I must go and wake him.'

'If he is asleep,' Andros said, 'then Marta and Mayrim can wake him up.'

Yeshua looked at the Twelve. 'Eleazar is dead.'

The disciples gasped. 'What?'

'I am glad – for your sake – that I was not there,' the Teacher said. 'Now you will truly believe. But we must leave and go to him.'

After walking for days through the parched land, they reached Bethany, the town where Marta and Mayrim lived. Bethany was two miles from Jerusalem and many people had come to comfort the sisters over the death of their brother.

Marta was in the main room of their house, sitting with Mayrim and some guests, when someone told her that Yeshua was coming to them followed by a large crowd.

'I will go and meet him,' Marta said.

When she reached the Teacher and his disciples, she fell into his arms, weeping.

'Yeshua, Teacher,' she said, 'I know that if you had been here, my brother would not have died.' She took a deep shuddering breath. 'But I still believe that YHWH will give you whatever you ask of Him.'

Yeshua let the woman weep for a moment longer and then, placing his hands on her shoulders, moved her where he could see her eyes. 'Your brother will rise again,' he said.

'I know,' she said, wiping her eyes with a cloth. 'He will rise in the resurrection on the last day, with all those who believe in YHWH.'

'I AM the resurrection,' Yeshua said, 'and the life. Whoever believes in me will live, even if he dies. And whoever lives and believes in me will *never* die.' He gazed at her intently. 'Do you believe this?'

Marta stared into Yeshua's eyes. 'Yes, Lord,' she said, 'I believe that you are the Messiah, YHWH's Son, whom the prophets said was coming.'

Yeshua nodded. 'Good. Where is your sister?'

'She is at the house. I will go and get her.'

'We will wait here,' Yeshua answered in a whisper.

Marta hurried back to the house. She leaned over her sister and whispered into her ear, 'The Teacher is here and is asking for you.'

Mayrim lifted red, grief-stricken eyes and looked at her sister. Then, with a sob, she stood and ran through the doorway.

'Where is she going?' one of the women asked.

'To the tomb, to grieve,' said another.

'We should go with her,' a third woman added.

As the women went out, they told the other mourners where they were going. Soon a large crowd followed Mayrim and Marta and were surprised to see the younger sister run up to Yeshua and fall weeping at his feet.

'Sir,' Mayrim cried, 'if you had been here, my brother would not have died.'

Tears filled the Teacher's eyes and flowed into his beard. He lifted his head towards the sky, his face wracked with sorrow.

'Where is his tomb?' he asked.

'Come,' Marta said, 'I will show you.'

The sisters and Yeshua – followed by the Twelve and the other mourners – walked to the edge of the town, where several caves in a rocky hillside were used as tombs. Some of the caves were natural, while others had been dug into the rock. Each had a large stone rolled in front.

Marta and Mayrim walked up to one of the caves. The markings in the ground in front of the tomb indicated that the large stone had recently been moved in place.

'This is where . . . Eleazar . . . was laid,' Mayrim said.

Yeshua wept.

'Look at him,' one man said. 'He must have cared deeply for Eleazar.'

Several people nodded in agreement.

'I have heard that the Teacher *healed* the blind,' said a woman. 'If he could do that, couldn't he have kept Eleazar from dying?'

Others nodded in agreement with her.

Yeshua walked up to the tomb, his eyes focused on the stone slab that covered the doorway. He laid a hand on the stone.

'Take this stone away,' he said.

A loud gasp rippled through the crowd. Marta looked at the Twelve and walked up to Yeshua.

'Sir, Eleazar has been dead for four days,' she said. 'The body will stink of death.'

Yeshua looked at her, his gaze piercing.

'Marta, didn't I tell you that if you believed, you would see YHWH's glory?'

She looked at him for a moment and then turned to the crowd. 'Would someone please remove the stone?'

No one in the crowd moved and then Cephas nodded to his brother and the other disciples. Walking to the tomb, they put their shoulders against the massive stone and pushed. A wheeze of air suddenly escaped the tomb as the stone moved, exposing the opening. Several minutes later, the stone was to one side of the dark entrance to the cave.

Yeshua walked up to the tomb. He lifted his head towards the heavens.

'Father,' he shouted, 'I thank You that You have heard me. I know that You always hear me, but I said this so that those standing here will hear and believe that You have sent me.' Lowering his face, Yeshua extended a hand towards the tomb's opening. 'Eleazar!' his voice echoed against the rocks. 'Come out!'

The crowd stood frozen for a moment. Then they looked at each other, shrugging their shoulders. Several giggled nervously. One of the women crossed to Marta and Mayrim.

'Come,' she said. 'Let's go back to the . . .'

'Look!' a woman screamed, pointing towards the tomb.

In the mouth of the tomb, stood a figure wrapped from shoulders to feet in white linen. It was shaking its head vigorously from side to side, until the white cloth fell from its face.

'Eleazar!' Mayrim cried and ran to her brother, followed closely by Marta.

'It's a miracle!' a man cried.

'Praise be to YHWH!' cried a woman. 'Yeshua truly is the Messiah.'

Yeshua turned to the Twelve, who were staring wide-eyed with shock. 'Take the grave wrappings off Eleazar and let him go.'

15

Anointed

'Marta, is it true?' a woman stopped her in the market. 'Is it true that Yeshua is coming here?'

Marta nodded. 'He sent word that he will go to Jerusalem for Passover and will stay with us for a while beforehand. Mayrim and I are preparing a meal in his honour and to give thanks that he brought our brother back to life: Eleazar's resurrection.'

Marta and Mayrim worked busily for several days, cleaning the house and preparing a banquet. Not only people from Bethany were invited, but also several of the priests from Jerusalem.

Marta was overjoyed with the evening. The food was plentiful and many guests said they had never eaten better. Marta did not complain – even in her heart – when Mayrim left the room shortly after the meal was finished. Since Eleazar's resurrection, the sisters' attitudes towards each other had changed. *If Mayrim is not here,* thought Marta, *then she is doing something important.* She carried the platter littered with crumbs of date and honey cakes out to the cooking area and then returned to the house.

She met Mayrim, who was about to enter the main room. Her younger sister was carrying an alabaster jar. The beauty of the white alabaster jar spoke of the purity and value of its contents. The mouth of the jar was sealed, protecting the nard inside.

Nard was expensive – one of the richest perfumes made – and their father had given each of his daughters a small alabaster jar filled with this rich perfume as part of their future dowry. They were to open these jars only to anoint themselves on their wedding day. They never removed these jars from their rooms and guarded them carefully.

'Mayrim, what are you doing?' Marta asked.

Her sister said nothing and headed purposefully into the main room. Marta followed as Mayrim walked round the low tables where the guests were reclining and knelt by Yeshua's feet.

A powerful fragrance filled the air as Mayrim broke the seal on the alabaster jar. Tipping the container, she poured the nard onto Yeshua's feet. The precious oil ran over his skin and between his toes before spilling onto the floor.

A soft gasp had rippled through the room when Mayrim broke the seal; the sound increased as Mayrim removed her head cloth and set it aside. She took a handful of her loosened hair and, picking up one of Yeshua's feet, she wiped the dripping perfume from it. She gently lowered the Teacher's foot again and then wiped the other foot.

Before Marta could take a step towards her sister, Juda jumped up. 'What do you think you are doing, woman?' he snapped. 'I cannot believe that your brother or sister allowed you to act in such a scandalous way. Beyond that, the nard is worth a fortune – more than a year's wages. If you didn't want to give the perfume to support the Teacher's work, then you should have sold it and given the money to the poor.'

Anger at Juda's comments overwhelmed the embarrassment that Marta felt for Mayrim. *Support the Teacher's work?* she thought. *Juda, you might look after the money for Yeshua, but my brother heard that you are a thief and have stolen from that money.* Before she could open her mouth, Yeshua stood, his eyes flashing with anger.

'Leave Mayrim alone,' he said. 'My Father intended her to save the perfume for this day. She was preparing me for my burial. There will always be poor people among you, but you will not always have me.'

Juda's face turned a deep red. He looked at Mayrim and then at Yeshua and then at the crowd. Walking to the door, he left the house, pushing past the crowd that had gathered outside in hope of seeing the Teacher.

He walked down the street, muttering to himself. As he passed the synagogue, he heard someone call to him. He looked up as several men dressed in priestly robes approached him.

'You are one of the Teacher's followers, are you not?' one of the priests asked.

Juda was so angry he couldn't speak; he nodded once in response.

'We understand some believe that he is the *Messiah*,' another priest said. 'We hear that some believe he will lead the people in rebellion against Rome and restore the land to the glory of King David's rule. I'm sure if he does that, *you* will be an important man.'

'Well, I can't say . . .' Juda began.

'We would like to meet him,' the first priest said. 'But we don't know how to get past the crowds. Perhaps you could help. We would be glad to . . . *thank* . . . you for your help. We would be most generous.'

Juda looked back towards the house, where the crowd still gathered, and then at the priests. 'Tell me what you want,' he said.

16

The Announcements

A campfire snapped and danced, casting shadows on the men's faces while providing warmth against the evening's chill. Beyond the firelight a black snake slithered up a tree. A fat rat followed the reptile. They studied the Twelve sitting around the fire, listening to Yeshua.

'There He is, Wormwood,' the snake hissed disdainfully, 'teaching His *disciples.*'

'They appear to be listening intently, Lucifer,' the rat commented. 'I wonder what He is saying?'

'Move closer and listen,' Lucifer said. 'A rat won't attract much attention. Not like a cobra.'

The rat hunched down and scurried closer to the campfire. After several minutes, it returned.

'He was asking them who the people thought He was,' Wormwood said.

'And what did they answer?' Lucifer asked.

'One said, "People think you are Yochanan the Baptizer,"' his minion responded. 'Another said, "Some think you are Elijah or one of the prophets."'

'Was that all?' Lucifer asked.

'No,' Wormwood said. 'Then He said, "Who do you think I am?"'

'And what did they say?'

'The human called Cephas said, "You are the *Messiah*,"' the rat gulped and added, '"the Son of *YHWH*." And He told them not to tell anyone.'

'So,' the snake hissed, 'the humans are beginning to realize *who* He is.' Lucifer closed his slitted eyes in thought. 'I will have to do something about that. Stay here, Wormwood.'

The cobra lifted itself to its full height. As the rat watched, the reptile's form grew fainter and fainter, until it looked like a wisp of smoke. The wisp floated towards the campfire and joined the smoke wafting above the dancing flames.

Yeshua looked at his disciples. 'I must tell you something,' he said and then paused, as if listening. 'Passover will be . . . special . . . this time.'

The Twelve looked at each other and then leaned in excitedly to hear what the Teacher would say. They were not prepared for his next words.

'While we are there, I am going to suffer many things,' he said. 'I will be condemned by the elders of our people, the chief priests and the teachers of Moses' Law. I will be . . .' he paused, staring into the flames, and took a deep breath, '. . . *killed* . . . and after three days, I will come back to life.'

The Twelve gasped, staring at Yeshua as if paralysed. A wind blew through the campfire, causing the flames to spark and dance higher and the smoke to blow around the disciples.

'No!' Cephas jumped up and crossed over to grab Yeshua's arm. 'No!' he cried. 'You're wrong. You're the *Messiah*. You are to be the new King of Israel. This cannot happen to you!'

Yeshua looked first at his disciples' fear-stricken faces and then over Cephas's shoulder, where, dancing above the campfire, one particular wisp of smoke had the distinctive shape of a snake. A tendril from that wisp was lingering around Cephas's head.

Yeshua shook off Cephas's hand and, stepping back, lifted a hand to point at his disciple.

'Get away from me and mine, *Lucifer*!' he commanded. 'You are a hindrance to me. *That* is what men would want, but it is not what my Father wants.'

Whoosh!

The wind whipped the fire upwards, shooting sparks and smoke. The disciples jumped up to avoid being singed as the wind pulled the flames higher than a man – hissing and screaming in fury – and then . . . stopped.

The Twelve stared slack-jawed and wide-eyed at the campfire, which had returned to its gently dancing flames. As one, their heads swivelled to stare at Cephas and Yeshua; the Teacher appeared unaffected by what they had just witnessed.

Yeshua looked at Cephas and then at his other disciples. 'It's time to rest,' he said. 'The path before us is hard.'

17

The Tax Collector

'Is that Levi?'

The disciple turned to see a man whose rich garments could not hide his diminutive height standing near the tax collectors' booth at the end of the market street. The short man waddled over to Levi with a half-smile.

Levi nodded. 'It is I, Zakkay,' he said.

Zakkay looked at the disciple's simple clothing. 'I almost did not recognize you,' he said. 'What are you doing in Jericho? And why are you dressed like that? The last time I saw you, you were wearing clothing that reflected your wealth.' He noticed the basket filled with flatbread, cheese, dates and almonds. 'Now you look as if you are an ordinary man and not Levi the tax collector.'

'I am no longer a tax collector,' Levi said.

'Ah,' Zakkay nodded, smiling slowly. 'I had heard rumours that you had left a thriving career to follow this *Teacher* everyone speaks of. But I dismissed them as ludicrous.'

'The rumours are true,' Levi said. 'I have followed Yeshua for three years now.'

The little man's eyebrows arched in surprise. 'Why?' he asked.

Levi smiled. 'Because he asked me,' he replied.

'What?' Zakkay stammered. 'You were one of the best tax collectors in Capernaum – one of the richest – and you gave it all up because this man *asked* you?'

Levi nodded.

'This sounds like an interesting story . . .' Zakkay led Levi to sit in the shade of a large sycamore-fig tree. 'Tell me about it.'

Levi shrugged. 'There's not much to tell,' he said. 'I was in Capernaum, sitting at the tax collectors' booth near the sea. Since Yeshua lived in the area, I had heard of him, I had even seen him, but I had never . . . spoken to him . . .'

'No need to explain to me,' Zakkay patted the air with his hands. 'If ordinary people will have nothing to do with us, why would a prophet want to speak with "an evil tax collector" such as you and me?'

'Can you blame the *ordinary* people?' Levi asked. 'We not only collected the taxes that Rome demanded, but we *added* on to them and *kept* the difference.' He put a hand on Zakkay's shoulder. 'Admit it, Zakkay: tax collectors are thieves.'

The short man looked around, but no one had overheard – even near the crowded marketplace, everyone avoided Zakkay, the chief tax collector. For a brief moment, there was a pained look in his eyes, but when he turned back to Levi, he grinned, shrugging his shoulders. 'Okay, if you must be so *honest*, we're thieves for Rome.'

'I don't know about you, Zakkay,' Levi continued, dropping his hand from Zakkay's shoulder, 'but as I watched the people walking up and down the streets, greeting each other, laughing with each other, I realized *I* was the one who was poor. All the money I possessed could not fill the *emptiness* I felt inside. One day, I was counting the coins from the day's collection, when a shadow fell across the table. I looked up to see this new prophet – this Yeshua. He had stopped in front of my table and he was looking right *at me*. There was something in his gaze, as if he could *see* the loneliness I felt.

'I shook off that feeling and asked him what he wanted. He looked at me and said, "You. I want you to come with me and be one of my disciples." ' Levi laughed. 'I must have looked like a fish, gaping at him. I was sure I had misunderstood, that there was a mistake. Then I looked into his eyes and realized there was no mistake.' His face softened in memory. 'The Teacher wanted *me* – a despised tax collector – to become one of his special followers.'

'What did you do?' Zakkay asked.

Levi shrugged. 'I got up and left.' He laughed at the look of disbelief on Zakkay's face and grasped Zakkay's arm. 'I promise you, I have never once regretted that decision. My life has never been the same.'

'I'm sure it hasn't,' Zakkay said. 'You used to wear the finest of clothing and eat whatever you wanted. Now you wear poor clothing and eat simple food.'

Levi nodded. 'True,' he admitted, 'but I've never been without something to wear or eat. In fact, shortly after that day, I gave a banquet for Yeshua and his other close disciples – there are twelve of us now. I invited some of my *old friends* in the hope that they would feel as I did.'

Zakkay laughed. 'If they responded as you did, I'm certain Rome would hate it,' he said, 'which would make the priests and Pharisees happy.'

'Well, the priests weren't happy,' Levi admitted. 'When Yeshua arrived, I went to the door to greet him. There was a group of Pharisees standing nearby watching him – I think they are afraid of Yeshua taking away some of their influence over the people.

'These Pharisees called out to Yeshua, asking him why a man who claimed to follow YHWH would "eat with tax collectors and sinners".'

'What did this Yeshua say?'

Levi laughed. 'He said, "Healthy people do not need a physician. I have come to call the sinners – not those who are righteous – to repentance."'

Zakkay laughed along with Levi. 'I wish I could have been there,' he said. 'Someday I would like to meet this Yeshua.'

'You can,' Levi said. He looked around and then lowered his voice. 'He and the other disciples are outside Jericho. Wherever he goes now, people crowd around him. I have come into town to buy some food. Come with me, Zakkay. I know Yeshua would love to meet you.'

The little man stopped smiling. He stepped back, shaking his head. 'I can't, Levi,' he said. 'Yeshua may have accepted you, but you were one of many tax collectors. I am the chief tax collector. I work directly with Rome. There is no way your Teacher would accept me.'

'You're wrong,' Levi insisted. 'I've got to return to Yeshua and the others with this food. I won't say anything to Yeshua about speaking to you. We'll come right past the tax collectors' booth later today. Watch for us; you'll be able to tell which one he is. If you change your mind, I'll introduce you.'

Zakkay watched his old friend walk up the street towards the gates to the city. *Levi . . . following a prophet*, he thought, shaking his head in disbelief. *Who would have thought that would ever happen?*

He tried to concentrate on work, but his thoughts kept drifting to Levi and this Yeshua. If ever someone had changed like night into day, it was Levi. He used to be a shrewd and merciless businessman who would collect the taxes Rome required while still making a tidy profit. And if it meant that some poor farmer or merchant lost their home or animal or business, Levi would shrug and comment, 'That's not my problem.'

After trying to count the day's collections three times without coming to the same sum, Zakkay swept the coins into a leather bag with a frustrated sigh, wrapped the strings around its mouth several times before knotting them, and dropped them in a special inner pocket in his robe. The evening promised to be pleasantly cool. He would just go home early, tell his servant prepare a special meal and serve it on the rooftop where Zakkay could enjoy the night breezes.

A noise drew his attention down the street. A large crowd were walking in his direction. People were cheering and laughing – and everyone talking at once – which drew other people who ran to see what the revelry was all about. Listening to people as they passed him, Zakkay caught snatches of conversation.

'Yeshua did what?'

'He healed a blind man! You know – the one who sat by the road at the city gates.'

'How did it happen?'

'From what I heard, a group of people followed Yeshua, cheering. The blind man asked someone what the commotion was all about and he was told that Yeshua, the prophet from Nazareth, was coming to Jericho.'

'Then this blind man started yelling for Yeshua, crying, "Have mercy on me!"'

'People around the man tried to hush him, but he only shouted louder, "Yeshua, please! Have mercy on me."'

'Then what happened?'

'Then Yeshua stopped and asked for the man be brought to him.'

'And then Yeshua asked the man, "What do you want from me?"'

'"Sir," the blind man said, "I want to see."'

'Then Yeshua said, "All right, because of your faith, you can see."'

'Truly, this Yeshua is a prophet from YHWH. For only a prophet sent from God could do these miracles.'

Zakkay stood frozen as the people surged past him, all talking about the miracle that had just occurred. *This Yeshua is Levi's friend. He has healed a blind man; he has healed the loneliness in Levi's life. I must see this man,* he thought.

Someone in the crowd called out, 'There he is! Yeshua is coming this way! Hurrah! Yeshua is coming this way!'

From the location of the cheer and the path it followed in the crowd, Zakkay was able to determine where Yeshua was. The little man tried to worm his way through the crowd; but no one would let him through. He began jumping, trying to see over the heads of the people in front of him but he was too short.

The movement of the crowd forced him against the sycamore-fig tree where he had sat with Levi. He looked up, his hand stroking his beard and thought furiously. He had to do something soon or he would miss Yeshua. Suddenly, he focused on the tree, with its thick, low-hanging branches. After a moment, he nodded to himself.

Leaning over, Zakkay grabbed the back hem of his robe and pulled it up between his legs, tucking it into the belt. He squatted down and then jumped up, grabbing the lowest branch. He hung there for a moment, adjusting his grip until he felt secure. Then he swung his legs up and wrapped them around the branch, pulling himself up. The gold braid on his robe caught on the tree's bark, ripping the costly trim, but for once Zakkay didn't care.

He stood up on the branch, holding on to the trunk and a branch overhead for balance. He was thankful that leaves provided a good covering. *You would have to know I was here to see me*, he said to himself. Leaning over, he watched for Levi and Yeshua.

Soon, the crowd under the tree began to cheer. *He's here,* Zakkay thought. *He's here!*

The crowd underneath the tree parted, allowing a group of men to pass. Zakkay spotted Levi who was looking over the crowd in the direction of the tax collectors' booth. Then he saw the familiar figure of the blind man, dressed in filthy rags. Only his eyes were no longer covered in the white film of blindness, but were clear and sparkling as he jumped and shouted. Zakkay looked at the younger man walking beside the blind man and felt his mouth go dry.

This is Yeshua, he thought. *There is* something about him, *just like Levi said. And he just healed a blind man. If he could do that, maybe he could* . . .

'Zakkay.'

The tax collector jumped at the sound of his name. He wobbled and grabbed the tree trunk with both hands. Then he looked down.

Yeshua had stopped and was looking *straight up at him* and smiling.

The little man noticed that everyone else in the crowd was staring at him as well, and none of them were smiling. With the exception of Levi, from their expressions it was obvious they were all expecting the prophet to call down fire – like Elijah – to consume him. Zakkay closed his eyes and waited.

'Zakkay, you must come down right now,' Yeshua said. 'I must stay at your house today.'

What? Zakkay's eyes popped open to see Yeshua – and Levi – grinning at him. He needed no other encouragement. He scrambled down the tree, heedless of his rich fabric robe.

As he walked through the crowd, he noticed that the response towards the Teacher had changed. Even when he was standing in front of the Teacher, the people – who moments before had been cheering over his healing a blind man – were now muttering among themselves, questioning Yeshua. 'What kind of *holy man* would be the guest of such a sinful man as Zakkay?'

On a different day, Zakkay would have been embarrassed and angry over such comments. But looking into the gentle, smiling eyes of Yeshua, Zakkay realized that today was different. Someone *cared* about him. Never again would he feel the ache of loneliness and rejection. He felt like he was a new person and it was all because of Yeshua.

'Sir,' Zakkay said to the Teacher, 'right now I give half of my wealth to the poor.'

That comment turned the crowd's murmurs into startled gasps. Yeshua said nothing; he just kept smiling at the little man. Zakkay smiled back. *He felt so clean!*

'If I have cheated anyone,' he continued, 'I will pay back more than what the Law of Moses requires. Instead of replacing the amount plus interest, I will pay back four times the amount.'

The crowd's stunned silence erupted into cheers. People danced, people clapped their hands, people patted Zakkay on his back. All the while, Yeshua continued to smile at him.

'Today, salvation has come to you and your house,' the Teacher said to him. 'You have been restored to a right relationship with YHWH. For the Messiah has come to seek and to save those who were lost.'

18

The Arrival

The wind stirred whirlwinds of dust that danced across the road. The rat coughed and scratched its ear before scurrying after the black snake slithering across the road to hide in the shade of a large rock.

'He should be coming this way soon,' the snake hissed, peering down the road.

'How do you know?' the rat asked.

'I have other followers besides you, Wormwood,' the reptile snapped. 'They told me that He is going to Jerusalem for Passover. They also said that every day larger and larger crowds are following Him. I don't know what *the Creator* is planning to do, but I have to stop Him once and for all.'

'How are you going to do that, Lucifer?'

'I don't know yet,' the snake said, scanning the horizon. 'But, when He passes by, keep your eyes and ears open. Something may suggest itself to one of us.'

* * *

'Marta, that was a wonderful meal,' Yeshua said.

'Thank you, Teacher,' Marta said, refilling the Teacher's cup with water and wine. ' But I am not solely responsible. Miriam from Magdala and my sister Mayrim helped to prepare the meal.'

The other two women were also helping serve the meal. Marta's sister held a plate of warmed flatbread while Miriam from Magdala offered cheese and dates to the men sitting around the table.

'Then thanks to all you ladies,' Yeshua said.

Marta placed a pitcher of water and wine nearby. 'If you will excuse us, we will leave you gentlemen to finish your meal. Teacher, if we are going to travel with you and your disciples to Jerusalem, there are things we women need to buy in the marketplace.'

After the women left, Yeshua and the Twelve talked with their host Eleazar about everyday things – weather, family, acquaintances – while they finished the meal. When they had finished eating, Yeshua turned to Thaddai and Taoma.

'We will be leaving Bethany for Jerusalem later today,' he said. 'Thaddai and Taoma, I want you to go ahead of us. When you enter the village of Bethphage, you will find a young donkey – one that has never been ridden – tied there. Untie it and bring it to me.'

'What?' Taoma asked. 'Just walk up and untie an animal that doesn't belong to us?'

Yeshua nodded. 'I understand. If anyone asks you what you are doing, tell them that I need it.'

'May I ask why you need a donkey?' Thaddai asked.

Yeshua looked at his disciples. 'I want to ride it into Jerusalem.'

The Twelve stared at the Teacher and then at each other. 'It's the fulfilment of the prophecy from Zechariah,' Andros whispered in awe:

> *Rejoice greatly, O Daughter of Zion!*
> *Shout, Daughter of Jerusalem!*
> *See, your king comes to you,*
>   *righteous and having salvation,*
> *gentle and riding on a donkey,*
>   *on a colt, the foal of a donkey.'*

'Yeshua, are you going to proclaim yourself as the Messiah during this Passover?' Juda asked.

'I am going to do what I was called to do,' the Teacher said to the disciple, 'just as you must do the same.'

Juda frowned in confusion and started to speak, but was interrupted by a joyous explosion in the room. Thaddai and Taoma ran from the house while the other disciples shouted, laughed and danced around the room, clapping their hands on each other's backs and shoulders.

'At last!' Cephas shouted. 'You will become the new King of Israel and drive the Romans from our land.'

'To be free at last from foreign oppression,' Philippos said, wiping tears of joy from his eyes.

'To think that we would live to see Israel restored to the glory of King David's reign,' Netanel said.

There was a large crowd of people waiting outside. They had become followers of Yeshua and were travelling to Jerusalem to celebrate Passover with the Teacher and the Twelve. As Yeshua began walking from Bethany towards Jerusalem, the disciples told the news to some of the crowd near them. By the time they reached the small village of Bethphage, Yeshua's announcement had spread like wildfire through the crowd.

Thaddai and Taoma met them, leading a small donkey accompanied by its mother. The men interrupted each other in their excitement.

'It was just as you said, Teacher,' Taoma said, his eyes wide.

'We found the donkey and her colt tied to a post just after we entered the village,' Thaddai said.

'We untied them, just as you told us,' Taoma added.

'And some people came up, just as you said they would,' Thaddai said.

'They asked us what we were doing,' Taoma smiled.

'And we said, "Yeshua, the Teacher, needs them,"' Thaddai laughed.

'And they let us take them,' Taoma was laughing as well.

Cephas pulled off his cloak and threw it over the colt's back. 'Yeshua can sit on my cloak.'

'He can use mine as well,' Yochanan cried, removing his cloak. 'The next King of Israel needs something soft to sit upon.'

Yeshua climbed up on the young animal and gently patted its neck. He then straightened up and turned his face in the direction of Jerusalem.

Yaakov pulled a large palm branch from a tree and waved it over the Teacher's head. 'If the Romans can give palm branches to their conquering heroes, we can do no less for our new king.'

The crowd responded as well. Some removed their cloaks and spread them on the ground in front of the two donkeys – after the animals had passed, they would pick up their garments and run to the front of the crowd. Others stripped branches from palm trees and waved them as Yeshua passed by or spread them on the road before him.

Jerusalem was filled with pilgrims who had come to the city to celebrate Passover and the noise of the crowd approaching from Bethphage drew their attention. By the time Yeshua rode through the city gates, the streets were packed with people whose excitement had reached fever pitch.

'Hosanna – praise to YHWH!' a man yelled, waving his palm branch. 'Hosanna! He has sent the Messiah to save us!'

'YHWH has blessed us!' cried another. 'Praise the next King of Israel!'

These cheers echoed throughout the city, drawing some of the priests and leaders from the temple to the street where Yeshua was riding the donkey. When they saw the wild jubilation of the crowd and heard the cries of praise, they drew their priestly garments around them, bristling with anger.

'Teacher,' one of the Pharisees cried out. 'This is not proper. Tell these people to stop saying these things about you!'

Yeshua looked at the man. 'Let me tell you something,' he said. 'If these people were to be quiet, the stones would cry out instead.'

Cephas, who had overheard this exchange, looked at his brother and Yochanan. 'Do you understand what he meant by that?'

The other men shook their heads. 'No,' Yochanan replied. 'But then, I do not always understand everything Yeshua says.'

Andros shrugged his shoulders. 'Right now, I do not care whether I understand.'

The three men grinned in agreement and then turned to follow the donkey carrying Yeshua. As they were approaching Jerusalem, the Teacher stopped the animal.

Gazing upon the Holy City, Yeshua began to weep.

'Oh Jerusalem,' he cried. 'If only you had known that this day would bring you the *peace* you sought. Now it is hidden from your eyes. The days will come when your enemies will build an embankment around you. They will kill you and your children and will not leave one stone upon another, because you *did not recognize the time that YHWH came to you.*'

Yeshua sighed deeply and wiped his eyes. Then picking up the donkey's reins, he rode up the hill and through the city gate, into the very heart of Jerusalem.

Yeshua led the crowd through the streets until they were in front of the temple. He dismounted the donkey and patted the animal's head.

'Teacher,' Andros and Philippos walked up to him, with other men at their sides. 'These men approached us and asked to meet you.'

Yeshua looked at the men, who nodded in greeting. Taking a deep breath, he said, 'The hour has come for YHWH's Son to be glorified.'

An excited murmur rippled through the crowd. 'He's going to tell us how he plans to overthrow the Romans,' one person said. They gathered closer to hear him.

'Let me tell you something,' Yeshua continued. 'Unless a grain of wheat falls to the ground and "dies" – by germination – it remains only a seed. But if it dies, then it grows and produces more seeds.

'The man who loves his life – with all his earthly belongings – above everything else will lose it; but he who realizes that his earthly life – and his belongings – does not have value compared to an eternal life, will live forever.'

People in the crowd began to glance at each other, uncertain what the Teacher was saying.

'If a man wants to serve me, he must follow me, wherever I go. My Father will honour all those who serve me.'

Yeshua took a deep breath and let it out. 'My heart is troubled when I think about what I am facing. But what should I say? "Father, save me from all of this?" No, this was the reason that He sent me into this world. Instead, I will say, "Father, may your name be glorified!"'

The people were staring at him in confusion when suddenly a voice thundered from a clear blue sky. *'I have glorified it,'* the voice pealed across Jerusalem, *'and will glorify it again.'*

'Did you hear that thunder?' someone asked. 'It sounded almost like a voice speaking.'

'It was a voice speaking,' replied another.

'This voice was for your benefit, not mine,' Yeshua said. 'Now is the time for this world to be judged and the prince of this world to be driven out. However, when I am lifted up from the earth, many men will be drawn to me.'

Turning, he walked through the temple gate to the Court of the Gentiles, followed by the Twelve.

'Do you know what he meant?' someone in the crowd asked.

Everyone looked at each other and shrugged.

19

The Snake in the Temple

'Lucifer, isn't this the place where the humans worship *HIM*?' the rat asked, as he followed the snake alongside the wall of the temple.

'Yes,' the snake replied.

The rat shivered. 'Then why are we here? Won't He see us?'

'I have to take that risk, Wormwood,' the snake hissed. 'I must work out what He is going to do.' He slithered to hide near a bale of hay.

'I've never been here before,' Wormwood looked around. 'It reminds me of the place where the humans buy and sell things.'

'It is not much different,' the snake opened its mouth in a twisted parody of a smile. 'I worked hard to make it that way.'

The snake nodded his head in the direction of several tables. 'Do you see all those tables?' the reptile asked. 'Those humans sitting behind them are money changers. The Law that *HE* gave to Moses requires each of the

Hebrews to pay a temple tax. Many of them pay this tax during Passover.

'The humans in charge of the temple – through *my* suggestions – have added to that law by requiring this tax to be paid with special coins. The men at the tables not only change the ordinary coins for the special temple coins, they add a *special* fee to it.' The snake looked at his minion. 'They cheat the people just like the tax collectors who work for Rome.'

The sounds of animals bleating drew the rat's attention. 'What are all those cows and sheep and doves for?' it asked.

'Ah,' the snake hissed, 'that is my favourite part of the human worship. A blood sacrifice.

'These humans are to offer a blood sacrifice at special times of worship, including Passover. On this day, five days before Passover, a sacrificial lamb must be selected. Any animal they offer to *HIM* must be perfect, without any spot or disease. Those humans near the animals are inspectors who examine each animal to be sacrificed.'

The snake slithered closer to the pens where the animals were kept. 'The leaders of the temple have stated that the humans may buy one of their approved animals, or bring one of their own.'

'I get it now,' the rat squeaked. 'Those animals are never approved, so the humans end up having to buy one from the inspectors in the temple.'

'Yes,' the snake hissed. 'They buy them at an increased price, of course. And the inspectors and the money changers share their profit with the temple leaders.'

'What an excellent plan, Lucifer,' the rat giggled. 'The humans steal from each other, all in the name of worshipping *HIM*.'

'Be quiet!' the snake commanded. 'We must watch Him and His followers.'

20

The Last Days

It was later the same day, and the Twelve were wandering around the Court of the Gentiles. Some of them were queuing to pay their temple tax and others discussing which animal they should buy for the Passover meal. The explosive crash caused the Twelve to turn round. Each one knew what they would see. It was as if they had been fore-warned.

Yeshua was standing near a money changer's table, with coins scattered and spinning on the temple floor. Without hesitation, the Teacher strode to the next table and, grabbing the edge, overturned it. He ran to a merchant entering the court carrying cages of frightened doves and barred his way.

'Stop! Stop! Stop!' Yeshua cried in anger. 'The Holy Scriptures say, "My house will be called a house of prayer," but you have turned it into a den of thieves.'

The Pharisees who had watched the crowds cheering Yeshua when he entered Jerusalem came running into the Court of the Gentiles. After glancing at the chaos, they turned to each other in shocked anger.

'First, this man allowed the people to proclaim him as the Messiah,' said one of the priests.

'What if he *is* the Messiah?' asked a younger priest. 'Think of the miracles he has performed.'

'Surely you do not believe that this Galilean is the Messiah!' snapped another Pharisee.

'You are young, but you know what the ruling council – the Sanhedrin – would do if they heard you. They would put you out of the temple; you would lose your position of authority.'

The younger priest looked at his companions and then stared at the ground. 'I– I didn't say that Yeshua *was* the Messiah.'

'That's right,' the older Pharisee said. Then he gestured towards the Teacher who was still confronting the money changers, whose profits were scattered over the temple floor. 'Now there is this.' He swept his hand towards the crowd. 'Something *must* be done.'

He crossed the floor to confront Yeshua. 'Look at what you've done!' he cried. 'Who gave you the authority to do all these things?'

Yeshua glanced at the money changers, who were frozen in fear and confusion. Then he turned to face the older priest. 'I will ask you one question,' he said. 'If you answer me then I will tell you who gave me the authority to do these things. The baptism of Yochanan – was it from YHWH or from men?'

The older man's eyebrows wrinkled in confusion. He turned and walked a short distance away, gesturing for the other priests to follow him. When they had gathered around him, he whispered, 'What do you think? If we say that it was "From heaven", then the Teacher will ask, "Then why didn't you believe him?"'

'But do we dare say it was "from men"?' asked the younger priest. 'The people believed that Yochanan the Baptizer was a prophet sent from YHWH. If we deny his authority, who knows what the people will do?'

The priests whispered for several more minutes and finally turned back to glare at Yeshua. The older priest wrapped his rich robes around him and lifted his chin.

'We do not know,' he said.

Yeshua stared at the priests. 'Then I will not tell you where I get the authority to do these things.' Turning, the Teacher left the temple court, with the Twelve following.

Juda was the last disciple to leave the courtyard. He hesitated and turned to take a step towards the priests.

'Juda!' Andros had stepped back into the gateway to the court. 'Come on!'

Juda looked at the priests for a moment longer and then turned to follow Andros.

'Do something about Yeshua!' A money changer yelled at the priests, his words overheard by everyone standing around.

21

The Betrayal

The Court of the Priests was an impressive rectangular room, constructed from white marble decorated with plates of gold. There were large arched doors on the two long sides of the room. In the centre was an altar of uncut stone with a ramp that connected the top of the altar with the temple floor. Near the altar was a laver in which the priests could wash. Around the room were rings, hooks and tables; these, along with the altar, were all stained dark from the blood sacrifices. Wisps of smoke drifted over the altar from that day's sacrifices.

The leading men who made up the Sanhedrin – the supreme religious body in the land of Israel – were standing here and there in the Court of the Priests. The president of the council – along with his assistant – known as the 'father of the court' – stood at the top of a set of stairs leading to the Holy Place, which housed the Altar of Incense and the Holy of Holies.

The Holy of Holies was a perfect square. In it was placed the Ark of the Covenant. The high priest entered the Holy of Holies once a year on the Day of Atonement, when he offered a sacrifice for the whole nation of Israel. Separating the Holy of Holies from the rest of the temple was a thick curtain woven of fine linen and embroidered with pictures of cherubim – angels who stood in the presence of YHWH.

'Why has a meeting of the Sanhedrin been called?' asked Yosef, a wealthy council member from Arimathea. 'It is a matter of days until we celebrate Passover and there are things to be done. What is so important that it could not wait until later?'

'We are here to discuss the teacher Yeshua, from Galilee,' the president announced.

A murmur rippled through the gathering; 'problem', 'miracles', 'troublemaker', 'healing', echoed against the white marble walls.

The president listened, nodding his head. 'Yes,' he said, 'we've all heard the stories about this man, each one more amazing than the last. And I'm certain that by now you've all heard about what he did in the Court of the Gentiles.'

Heads nodded all around the room.

'He has insulted us, defied our authority,' the man who held the position of father of the court said, 'and now there are many people who believe he is the Messiah. If we let him continue like this, soon all will believe in him and then the Romans will come and take away our authority and our nation.'

'There is nothing we can do,' one of the priests said.

'He should be put to death,' said Annas, an elderly priest who commanded respect as a former high priest.

'But he has done nothing to warrant death,' argued Yosef.

'You know nothing,' said Caiaphas, the son-in-law of Annas, as he mounted the steps, accompanied by the two leaders of the Sanhedrin. Caiaphas was a member of the Sanhedrin as well as the high priest of the temple of YHWH for that year. He raised his arms to get everyone's attention. 'Do you not realize that it is better that one man dies for all the people than for the whole nation to perish?'

'Sirs?' a temple servant stood in the arched door. 'There is a man who wishes to speak with you.'

'He had better be someone of importance,' the president growled. 'I told you not to interrupt us.'

'He said you had spoken with him before about a certain . . . *problem* . . . you had,' the servant said. 'The man's name is Juda.'

The president's jaw dropped in surprise. He looked at the father of the court, whose eyes were wide with shock. The president looked at Caiaphas, who nodded and then turned to the temple servant.

'We will meet with him,' he said and then passed between the council members to step through the arched door into the Court of the Women.

A solitary man stood at the top of the stairs that led to the large court where all people – men and women alike – could enter. He was admiring the gilt on the wall and turned when he heard their footsteps.

'Sirs,' he said, looking around to make certain they were not overheard. 'Thank you for meeting me.'

The president nodded his head. 'Please explain your reason for speaking with us,' he said. 'As the servant no doubt told you, the Sanhedrin are in a meeting.'

Juda looked at the other men. 'You spoke with me once about Yeshua,' he said. 'You said you wanted information about him.'

The president said nothing, but nodded for Juda to continue.

'No doubt you've heard that many believe him to be the Messiah who will overthrow Rome's rule of Israel.' Juda took a deep breath. 'I *hate* Romans! I will do whatever is needed to see them thrown out of Israel. I followed Yeshua because I thought eventually he would drive the Roman pigs from our land.' He paused. 'I no longer think Yeshua wants to fight the Romans; but with the proper . . . *encouragement*, I think he might change his mind.'

'And you think that the Sanhedrin could provide this encouragement?' Caiaphas said.

Juda nodded.

The three Council leaders looked at each other.

'But Yeshua is always surrounded by his followers,' the president said. 'We would need to . . . get him alone . . . in order to speak with him. Could you help us do this?' When Juda hesitated, the president added, 'We could offer you something for your efforts.'

A sudden breeze blew through the Court of the Priests, blowing snake-like wisps of smoke to drift around the heads of the three priests and Juda. The disciple blinked as if to clear the smoke from his eyes; then his expression changed, growing sharp as a knife's blade.

'What will you give me if I hand him over to you?' Juda asked bluntly.

Caiaphas's eyes widened. Turning, he gestured to the other men. They stepped away to speak quietly with each other, then, reaching inside the pockets of their robes, brought out small bags that clinked. After rapidly counting the coins, the temple leaders turned back to Juda.

'We will give you thirty silver coins.'

Juda held out his hand. 'I'll take it.'

22

The Last Meal

'It is almost time for the Passover meal,' Taoma said. 'Our families and all the others who followed you into Jerusalem, have been asking where you will celebrate.'

Yeshua and the Twelve were staying with Eleazar and his two sisters. 'It is important that I celebrate this Passover, with only you twelve,' Yeshua said. 'Cephas, you and Yochanan go to Jerusalem. When you enter the city, you will find a man carrying a jar of water . . .'

'A *man* carrying water?' Cephas said. 'That is something only women do.'

'Then he will be easy to recognize, won't he,' smiled the Teacher. 'Follow this man; he will lead you to a house. Go to the owner of that house and say, "The Teacher says, 'My time is near. I want to celebrate the Passover with my disciples at your house. Where is the guest chamber that has been prepared?'" He will show you a large upper room, already furnished. Prepare the meal there. The rest of us will meet you there soon.'

Cephas looked around. 'Where is Juda?' he asked.

Yeshua closed his eyes and sighed. 'Juda is preparing for what he must do,' he said solemnly.

When Yeshua and his disciples – including Juda – arrived at the upper room, they found everything ready. Juda was agitated as if his heart was on fire. The moonlight streaming in through the windows and the flickering light from the oil lamps cast soft shadows around the room. Pillows scattered beside a long low table where the men would recline while eating were the only furnishings in the room. Serving platters and bowls were set around the table, filled with unleavened bread, vegetables, herbs, a sauce and the lamb that had been sacrificed earlier that day, then roasted. There were pottery cups set for each diner and several jars filled with wine placed near the centre of the table.

'Ah, Cephas, Yochanan, you have done well,' Yeshua said. Turning to include all the Twelve, he said, 'I have been anxious to eat this Passover meal with you before I must suffer. For this will be the last time I eat it until what this meal represents has occurred in YHWH's kingdom.' Yeshua sat at one end of the table, which was the position for the head of the family. The disciples selected their places, Juda on one side of Yeshua and Yochanan on the other. The meal followed the traditions that had been set down for generations. The disciples searched for any leavened bread that might be hidden in the room and then observed the ritual hand washing. The first of the four cups of wine were poured and Yeshua spoke the first prayer, 'Blessed are you, YHWH, Creator and King of the Universe, who has created the fruit of the vine . . . And you, YHWH, have given us festival days for joy; this feast of the unleavened bread, the time to remember our deliverance from Egypt. Blessed are you, YHWH, for you have kept us alive, sustained us, and helped us to enjoy this season.'

They ate the bitter herbs to remember the suffering their ancestors had undergone. Every eye looked through the lamplight to Yeshua. He seemed subdued as if the weight of the world pressed upon him.

The youngest – Yochanan – asked the traditional question, 'Why are we doing this?' to which Yeshua replied with a reminder of what all the Israelites had gone through as slaves in Egypt and how YHWH had delivered them through Moses. Holy Scripture was recited and hymns were sung. Then, there was a second hand washing, in preparation for the serving of the Passover Lamb and the unleavened bread. After the prayers of blessing and thanksgiving, they all began to eat, turning to their neighbours to talk in small groups.

'Yeshua is going to rally the people to attack the Romans,' Shimon said.

'That's what you *hope*,' Yaakov smiled. 'Once a zealot, always a zealot.'

'Well, if he is the *Messiah*, how else is he going to restore the kingdom?' Shimon asked. 'The Romans are not going to leave without a fight.' He looked around and lowered his voice, 'And I bought several swords, just in case.'

'You bought swords?' Cephas asked. 'Without asking me?'

'Why should I ask you?' Shimon folded his arms and glared at the big fisherman.

Cephas folded his arms and glared at the other disciple. 'Because I am the head of the Twelve.'

'When did this happen?' Netanel asked.

'What do you mean?' Cephas said. 'I was the first disciple Yeshua called.'

'Oh really?' Andros frowned. 'As I recall, I took you to meet him. I was with Yochanan the Baptizer; he told me to follow Yeshua and to meet him. So, I was actually the first.'

'Well, Yochanan and I are his cousins,' Yaakov said. 'That makes us closer to Yeshua than you.'

'What are you talking about?' Yeshua asked, his voice echoed over the room, silencing the arguments. The disciples reacted like young boys caught fighting over a favoured toy; they hunched their heads and refused to meet Yeshua's eyes.

'The kings of the earth rule over their subjects,' Yeshua said, 'but that is not how it is in my Father's kingdom. Let him who would be first take the last place. I am here amongst you as one who serves.'

Yeshua stood up and crossed the room to a small bench placed near the door. On it was placed a bowl, a pitcher of water and a large towel. He removed his outer robe and laid it aside. Taking the large towel, he folded it lengthwise and tied it around his waist. He then poured some water into the bowl and carried it over to the end of the table, where Levi sat.

While his disciples watched in shocked silence, Yeshua knelt and, lifting Levi's feet, he removed the disciple's sandals and placed his feet in the bowl. He scooped the water with his hands to pour over Levi's feet, rinsing off the dirt from the road. Then taking the towel wrapped around his waist, the Teacher dried Levi's feet. After replacing Levi's sandals, he straightened and crossed to the opened window to pour out the dirty water. Then he carried the bowl back to the bench to pour in fresh water.

One by one, Yeshua washed his disciples' feet. Their reactions varied to seeing the Teacher perform a job assigned to the lowest of servants. Some were silent with shock; some were too embarrassed to even look at him. When Yeshua knelt before Cephas, the big fisherman exploded with outrage.

'Teacher, what are you doing?' he demanded.

Yeshua looked at him. 'You don't understand now, Cephas,' he said, 'but one day you will.'

'No!' Cephas jerked his feet back from the Teacher's hands. 'You will *never* wash my feet!'

'If I do not wash you,' Yeshua said quietly, 'then you have no part with me or my kingdom.'

Cephas' eyes grew wide; his mouth gaped like a fish. Awkwardly, he stuck his foot out. 'Then, wash not only my feet,' he said, 'but also my hands and head.'

Yeshua smiled at his impetuous disciple. 'No,' he said. 'If you have bathed, all that is needed is to wash the dust from your feet, for you are clean.' He paused slightly and added, 'But not all are,' glancing at Juda.

After the last foot was dried and the bowl emptied, Yeshua put on his outer robe and took his place at the table. 'Do you understand what I just did?' he asked, looking around at his disciples. 'You call me "Teacher" and you are right; I am. If I, as your teacher, took on the role of a servant and washed your feet, then you ought to do the same for each other. You will be blessed if you do.'

Yeshua took a deep breath. 'But I am not speaking about all of you.' He closed his eyes, furrowing his brow as if in pain.

Yochanan placed his hand on Yeshua's arm. 'Are you all right?' he asked.

Yeshua sighed before opening his eyes. 'I must tell you something.' He looked around the table. 'One of you will betray me.' He raised his voice to be heard over the gasps from his disciples. 'I will go and do what is required of me, but woe to the man who betrays me.'

The disciples straightened, pulling away from the table. They glanced at each other, trying to determine the look of a traitor in the eyes of the men they had lived with for the past three years.

Andros leaned over to whisper to his brother, 'Cephas, what do you think he means?'

Cephas shrugged his shoulders. 'I don't know,' he whispered, 'but I'm going to find out one thing.' Leaning towards the Teacher, he asked. 'Yeshua, is it me?'

One by one, the other disciples asked Yeshua the same question.

Yochanan leaned in to whisper to his cousin. 'Yeshua, I am your family. You can tell me. Who is it?'

Yeshua tore off a piece of flatbread. 'I will dip this piece of bread into the sauce and hand it to the man.' He dipped the bread into the bowl of sauce and, turning, handed it to Juda.

Juda, sitting on the other side of Yeshua, had overheard what the Teacher had said to Yochanan. He looked from the bread extended to him, into the eyes of Yeshua. He took the bread, staring at him in disbelief. 'Is it me?' he asked.

Yeshua looked at him. 'You have said it,' he answered in a whisper.

Juda shook his head. 'You don't understand, Yeshua,' he said. 'I only wanted to help you–'

'Whatever you are going to do,' Yeshua interrupted him, 'do it quickly.'

Juda stared at him wordlessly, his expression changing from disbelief to irritability to anger. Standing, Juda tossed the bread down on the table. Turning, he crossed to the door and left the room.

'Where is Juda going?' Thaddai asked. 'Is he going to buy something for the meal?'

'The meal is nearly over,' Taoma said. 'The Teacher probably sent him out to give some money to the poor.'

Yeshua sat up and faced the table; his disciples followed his example.

'Now will YHWH be glorified through His Son. I will be with you only a little longer and you will not be able to go with me.

'For now, I give you a new commandment. Love each other, just as I have loved you. This is how all men will know that you are my disciples, by the way you love each other.'

Lifting the flatbread from the platter in front of him, Yeshua raised it above his face and offered a prayer of thanksgiving. Then, he tore the bread in half and handed a piece to the disciples sitting on each side of him.

'Take this and eat it,' he said. 'This is my body, which is given for you. Whenever you do this, remember me.'

The disciples stared at each other in confusion, but did not question the Teacher. Ripping off a small piece from the flatbread, they handed it around the table.

After the last piece of bread came back to Yeshua, he lifted his cup of wine to bless it in the same way and then handed it to Yochanan. 'Drink all of this,' he said. 'This cup is the new covenant in my blood, which is poured out for you and for all mankind, in payment for your sins. Whenever you do this, remember me.'

When the cup came to Cephas, he took a sip from the cup and handed it to his brother. Then he turned back to the Teacher. 'Sir,' he asked, 'where are you going?'

'Where I am going you cannot come now,' Yeshua replied. 'Oh Cephas, Lucifer, the ancient adversary of your soul, has asked for all of you, to test you and sift you as if you were wheat. But I have prayed for you.'

'Yeshua, why can't I come with you?' Cephas asked. 'I am ready to go with you, whether it is prison or death. I would die for you.'

'You would die for me, Cephas?' Yeshua looked at him sadly. 'Before the cockerel crows twice, you will deny me three times. You will all abandon me tonight, just as the prophet wrote, "I will strike the shepherd and the sheep will be scattered." But when I am raised up, I will go ahead of you to Galilee.'

'No!' Cephas stood, his fist clenched. 'Even if everyone else denies you, *I* never will. I would die for you!'

'I would die for you!' Yochanan said. The other disciples also vowed they would die before betraying their Teacher.

'Please sit down,' Yeshua said to his disciples. When they had sat back down, he extended his hands towards them.

'Don't be troubled,' he said. 'Trust YHWH and trust me. In my Father's house are many rooms. I am going to prepare a place for you and will come back and take you with me, so that we may be together. You know the way to where I am going.'

Taoma spread his hands in confusion. 'Teacher,' he said, 'we don't know where you are going; how can we know the way?'

'I am the way,' Yeshua said, his voice filling the room, 'and the truth and the life. No man can come to know my Father unless he meets Him through me. If you really knew me, you would know my Father and, from now on, you will know Him.

'Teacher,' Philippos said. 'Show us the Father and that will be enough for us.'

'Do you not believe that I am in the Father, Philippos?' Yeshua asked. 'Believe me when I tell you that I am not saying these things from myself; whatever I say comes from my Father. Or, at least believe on the evidence of the miracles I performed.

'Let me tell you, that whoever has faith in me will do what I have been doing. He will do even greater things, because I am going to my Father. I will do anything that you ask that will bring glory to my Father.

'I have taught you many things while I was with you. But my Father will send you the Holy Spirit who will teach you and remind you of everything I said.'

Yeshua stood and moved to place his hands on Cephas's and Andros's shoulders. Lifting his eyes, he prayed, 'Father, the time has come. Glorify Your Son, that Your Son may glorify You. I have brought glory on earth by completing the work You sent me to do. You granted me authority over all people that I might give eternal life to all those You have given me. That eternal life is that they may know You, the only true God and Yeshua the Messiah, whom You sent.

'My prayer is not for them alone. I pray also for those who will believe in me through their message, that all of them may be one, Father, just as You are in me and I am in You. May they also be in Us so that the world may believe that You have sent me. May they be brought to complete unity to let the world know that You sent me and have loved them even as You have loved me.'

He looked at the disciples, whose eyes were filled with confusion and fear. 'I am leaving you peace,' he said. 'Not the peace that the world gives, but *my* peace. Don't let your hearts be troubled and don't be afraid. I have told you all of this before it happens so that after it happens, you will believe.'

Yeshua's face darkened. 'Lucifer, who considers himself to be the prince of this world, is coming. He has no authority over me, but the world must learn that I love my Father and do exactly what He tells me to do.' His grip tightened on his disciples' shoulders. 'Let me tell you, that what was written about me by the prophet will be fulfilled, "He will be considered one of the criminals."

'Come now,' he said. 'It is time to go.'

23

The Arrest

The night air blew cold and clammy against Juda's neck like the breath of a tomb. He hunched his shoulders and pulled his cloak closer. Few people would be outside during the Passover meal, but he hurried through the streets of Jerusalem, frequently looking around as if he expected attack. The buildings were dappled with shadows cast from the moon.

Juda turned up the road that led to the high priest Caiaphas's house. Several minutes later, a number of servants rushed from the house, bearing messages for the leaders of the Sanhedrin as well as the captain of the temple guard. Within the hour, a group of guards and servants left Caiaphas's house and followed Juda through the darkened streets.

'How will we know which one to arrest?' one of the guards asked.

'The man I greet will be him,' Juda said.

'Not good enough,' said the soldier. 'You could meet anyone on the streets and accidentally greet him.'

'Fine!' Juda snapped. 'The man whose cheek I *kiss* – *he* is the one.'

* * *

In a nearby street the rest of the Twelve followed Yeshua. He walked quickly, as if he had to meet someone. Never looking back, Yeshua walked faster and faster.

'Do you have any idea where we are going?' Andros asked his brother as the disciples followed Yeshua through the streets of Jerusalem.

Cephas shrugged. 'No,' he replied. 'When Shimon showed Yeshua the two swords he had and Yeshua said they were enough, I thought we were going to attack the Antonia Fortress.'

'What?' Andros whispered fiercely. 'Attack the Roman fortress when there are more than six hundred Roman soldiers there at all times? Were you expecting Yeshua to multiply those two swords like he did the loaves of bread and the fish?'

'No,' Cephas snapped. 'I thought he might have arranged for others to meet us. After all, Juda left the meal shortly after speaking with the Teacher.' Cephas looked at the buildings around them. 'It looks like he is leading us away from the city.'

Yochanan and Yaakov moved closer to Cephas and Andros. 'Do you understand anything about what Yeshua was talking of tonight?'

'Why does everyone think *I* know what the Teacher is thinking?' Cephas snapped.

'Well, earlier tonight you stated that you were the most important of the Twelve,' Yaakov retorted. 'We assumed that meant Yeshua would tell you of his plans.'

Cephas turned towards Yaakov, his fists balled; but Andros laid a hand on his brother's arm. 'Please, don't,' he said. 'No more fighting. Not after all Yeshua said to us. He's *leaving* us and we don't have much more time with him.'

Andros's words hit Cephas like a battering ram. He slumped, his heart jerking in his chest, and tears filled his eyes. 'Why would he leave us?' Cephas whispered. 'And why won't he take us with him?'

'I don't know,' Yochanan said. 'Since he was a child, Yeshua has always said and done things no one expected, but tonight the things he spoke about . . . he said we were all going to d-d . . .' The disciple couldn't speak the word aloud, but it echoed in each man's memory.

'Before the cockerel crows twice, you will deny me three times . . . You will all abandon me tonight . . . I will strike the shepherd and the sheep will be scattered.'

'Wait,' Yaakov said. 'He said that someone would strike the shepherd.' He looked at the others. 'Instead of us attacking the Antonia Fortress, do you think Yeshua knows of a plan to attack us?'

'Hmmm . . . maybe,' Yochanan said, nodding his head. 'Maybe that's why he is leading us away from Jerusalem. He is trying to hide.'

Cephas – his pride still stinging from the suggestion that he would do anything so cowardly as to *deny* his friend – squared his shoulders and clenched his fists. 'If we are going to be attacked,' he said, 'they will not surprise *me*.' Slowing his pace, he dropped back to speak quietly with Shimon and a moment later, took a sword from the other disciple and hid the weapon inside his cloak.

While the disciples were talking, Yeshua led them through the streets of Jerusalem, down the Kidron Valley near the eastern wall, to the slopes of the Mount of Olives. Here, at the foot of the hillside, was a small garden-like enclosure where an orchard of olive trees grew; the garden was called Gethsemane meaning 'olive press'. The Teacher loved Gethsemane and would often go there to relax, to meditate and to pray.

Yeshua stood in the midst of the garden, his disciples standing among the shadows of the olive trees.

'Sit here,' he said, 'while I go over there to pray. Cephas, Yochanan, Yaakov, you will come with me.'

Cephas turned to look at Shimon and touched his cloak. *'Keep watch,'* he mouthed to the other disciple, who nodded in return. He adjusted his cloak and crossed the short distance to follow Yeshua and the two brothers towards a clearing among the trees.

'Yeshua, what's the matter?' Yochanan held the Teacher's arm.

Cephas grasped the hilt of the sword and nearly pulled it from his cloak, until Yeshua said, 'I am so *sad*.'

'Sad?' Cephas asked, releasing the hilt and smoothing his cloak. 'What do you mean?'

'My soul is *overwhelmed* with sorrow to the point of death,' Yeshua said. 'I must pray for YHWH to give me strength to face what is before me. Please, stay here and keep watch with me. Pray that YHWH will give you the strength to resist the testing and temptation you are going to face.'

Cephas watched the Teacher walk over to the far side of the clearing. He looked at the other two disciples. 'What should we do?' he asked.

Yochanan shrugged. 'He said we should pray.' The two brothers adjusted their cloaks and knelt near several large tree stumps.

Cephas sighed. It was dark, it was late and his stomach was full; all he needed to fall asleep was to sit and be still. But, his Teacher and friend had asked him to pray and keep watch and that was exactly what he would do.

He looked to make certain the other two men had their heads bowed in prayer and then removed the sword from his cloak. He found a large rock and laid the sword next to it. Then, adjusting his cloak and robes to protect his knees from the sharp stones, he knelt. He reached down to determine that the sword was placed where he could reach it and practised grabbing it several times. When he was satisfied that he was ready, Cephas placed his elbows on the stone, clasped his hands and leaned his forehead against them. His breathing began to slow and – after a few minutes – his hands slipped. The disciple laid his head on the stone, snoring.

Yeshua paced around the small clearing, taking deep breaths and clutching his hands until his knuckles were white. Abruptly, he dropped to his knees, unconcerned that sharp stones might cut his legs and lowered his face to the ground.

'*Father,*' he groaned, 'my time is near. I understand what You want and I desire to do Your will above everything in my life. But, what I will have to face – what I will have to bear – is torturous. If there is *any other way* that Your purpose can be accomplished, please take this . . . *cup* . . . away from me.'

Yeshua continued his prayers, pouring out his heart to the One he knew loved him, to the One he trusted more than life.

After a while, he stood and walked to where he had left the three men. They were still leaning against the stones and stumps, but the slump of their bodies and their grinding snores revealed their true condition.

'Cephas,' the Teacher groaned, 'Yochanan, Yaakov!'

The three awoke, startled, shaking their heads, their eyes still dazed from sleep. 'Huh? What?'

'I asked you to pray with me,' Yeshua said. 'Could you not even stay awake?'

The three disciples were embarrassed to be caught asleep. They couldn't even bring themselves to look at their Teacher as they mumbled apologies.

Cephas was rigid with shame, tears misting his eyes – he'd forgotten about the sword. *It could have been anyone who woke us,* he thought, *and I completely forgot about the sword.*

'You must stay alert,' Yeshua said, 'and pray for the strength to resist what is about to happen. The spirit may be strong and have the right intentions, but the body is weak.' Turning, the Teacher walked back to the far side of the clearing.

The other disciples glanced at each other and silently adjusted their posture and clothing. Cephas was determined to find a position that would help him stay awake and pray. *If I do nothing else before he leaves*, he thought, *I will pray as Yeshua asked*. The thought of his friend leaving hit him afresh, overwhelming the big fisherman. He leaned his head against his hands, thankful that the night hid the tears that fell onto the stone. He wrestled with the memories of being with Yeshua and the looming years ahead without him.

Grief overwhelmed the men, yet soon – from the rock where Cephas prayed as well as the nearby stumps – the soft sounds of snoring filled the air.

On the far side of the clearing, Yeshua fell to his knees beside a large rock. 'Father, *My* Father,' he prayed, 'I know that everything is possible for You and You could take this . . . *cup* . . . from me. However, if it is necessary for this cup of Your wrath against sin to be poured out . . .' he paused and took a deep, trembling breath, 'then Your will be done. I will drink it.'

A breeze blew through the trees, carrying an unearthly voice. 'Isn't it tender how much He trusts His Father?' it said. 'Look at how He trembles. Look at how He is sweating. Wasn't that one of the curses the Creator placed upon the first man? To earn his bread by the sweat of his brow? But look,' the voice shook with an evil laugh, 'that is not sweat oozing from His skin: it is *blood.'*

The evil taunting was cut short with a pained squeal as a blinding light appeared in the clearing. At the centre of the light stood a figure, larger and taller than any human. Every inch of him pulsed with light – from the wild mane of hair to his spotless robe and breadth of his majestic wings. In one hand, the angel held a golden goblet and, in the other hand, a golden basket filled with bread, and over his arm was draped a white cloth.

The angel knelt in front of Yeshua. 'For the Son who obeys the will of the Creator,' his voice echoed like the sound of rushing water, 'strength, comfort and peace are given.'

After the angel left him, Yeshua walked back to the other side of the clearing and woke his sleeping friends once again. Their weakness mortified the three disciples, robbing them of excuses or apologies.

While his words strengthened their resolve, it was to no avail. Shortly after their Teacher left them, once more they fell asleep.

Returning to the other side of the clearing Yeshua knelt, lifting his face and hands towards heaven. 'Father, I am ready,' he said. 'May Your will be done in all the earth, that Your name may be glorified and honoured.'

Returning to wake his sleeping disciples the third time, the Teacher asked, 'Are you still sleeping?' He walked towards the entrance of the garden – Cephas, Yochanan and Yaakov stumbling after him – where he found the rest of the disciples sprawled on the ground asleep.

'Enough!' he said, as they heard the sound of footsteps approaching. 'The hour has come. Look, the Son of YHWH is betrayed into the hands of sinners. Get up! We must go! Here comes my betrayer!'

The disciples were shocked to see men enter the darkened garden and head through the trees towards them. Some were servants carrying torches and lanterns, and others wore the uniform of the temple guard and carried swords. What shocked the disciples even more was the man leading this contingent.

'Juda!' they gasped.

Cephas' eyes narrowed and he slipped his hand inside his cloak to wrap it around the hilt of the sword.

Juda hesitated, looking at his former companions, then stumbled as the captain of the guard shoved him forward. Frowning at the guard, he turned and slowly approached Yeshua.

'Greetings, Teacher,' he said; then he leaned over to kiss Yeshua's cheek.

He was startled when Yeshua whispered, 'Juda, you would betray me with a kiss?'

Juda opened and closed his mouth like a dying fish.

Before he could reply, Yeshua continued, 'Friend, do what you came for.'

The captain of the temple guard stepped forward brandishing his sword. 'You will come with me,' he said, grabbing Yeshua by the shoulder.

'No!' Cephas leaped towards the group of men, swinging the sword. 'Attack, Shimon!' he cried. 'For Yeshua! King of the Hebrews!'

'Aaaaaiiiii!' One of the servants dropped a lantern and grabbed the side of his face. The fire of flickered wildly in the lantern, casting shadows on the bloodied ear lying on the ground.

'He cut off Malchus's ear!'

The temple guards stepped forward, lifting their swords.

'No more of this!' Yeshua's voice echoed through the night sky.

The guards and disciples froze, with weapons lifted.

The Teacher pulled his arm from the man who held him and crossed to pick up the severed ear. Straightening up, Yeshua turned and gently placed the ear against the wounded man's head.

The man's moans stopped and his eyes widened. Lifting both hands, he felt the side of his face. 'It's all right!' he cried. 'My ear is healed!'

With a strangled cry, the guards fell to the ground looking from Malchus to Yeshua.

'Put your swords away,' Yeshua said to Cephas and Shimon. 'Those who depend upon swords will die by swords. Do you not realize that I could call on my Father and He would instantly place more than seventy thousand angels at my disposal? But how then would the prophecies in the Holy Scriptures be fulfilled?

Turning, he approached the captain of the temple guard. 'Who are you looking for?' he asked.

'Yeshua from Nazareth,' the guard said.

'I am he,' Yeshua replied. 'Do I look like I am leading a rebellion that you have come out with guards and swords to capture me? When I was teaching in the temple courts, you did not arrest me.'

The captain of the temple guard looked around, uncertain what to do next. It was obvious this man was not trying to lead a rebellion, but Caiaphas would be furious if he returned empty-handed.

Yeshua solved his dilemma. 'If you are looking for me, I'll go with you,' he said. 'But let my followers go.'

The captain nodded at Yeshua and gestured for another guard to bind the Teacher's arms.

'Yeshua of Nazareth,' he said, 'I am arresting you as a traitor against Rome.'

'No!' Juda cried, grabbing the captain's arm. 'That wasn't what was agreed upon! The penalty for treason against Rome is *death*.'

The captain shook off Juda's hand. 'You should have thought of that before you *betrayed* him,' he said.

The other disciples gaped at Juda.

'You *betrayed* Yeshua!' Cephas growled.

'Why would you do this?' Yochanan asked. 'What did he ever do to you?'

'No,' Juda pleaded, 'you don't understand. He was to be the next King of Israel. I wanted to help him.'

Taoma grabbed Juda's forearm.

'You helped him all right,' he said. 'If he is found guilty, they will *crucify* him.'

Juda shook off the disciple's hand. 'And you as well!' Juda retorted. 'You are his followers!'

The eleven disciples looked at each other as they realized what Juda had said. Turning, they fled through the garden, dodging trees and jumping over stumps and rocks.

'Look what I have here,' one of the guards laughed. He held up a man's robe. 'It belongs to one of *his* followers. When he ran past me, his robe caught on the hilt of my sword. Apparently, he thought I meant to arrest him as well. He raised his arms and slipped out of his robe. Somewhere, a follower of Yeshua is running through the night wearing *nothing*!'

The captain of the temple guard laughed. 'Well, Juda, it appears your friends weren't so . . .' he stopped and looked around. 'Where did Juda go?' he asked.

The guards looked around but couldn't find Juda.

'Well, it appears that not only have your friends deserted you,' the captain said to Yeshua, 'but even your *betrayer* didn't want to stick around.

'Come!' he ordered his men, 'The high priest will be waiting.'

Yeshua looked around as he was led away. Before they left the garden, he saw the snake wrapped around the bough of a tree. 'This is your hour, Lucifer,' he said, 'the hour when darkness reigns.'

24

The Trial

The torches around the courtyard cast an eerie dance of shadows on the walls of Caiaphas's villa, hinting at the evil that walks in the midnight hours.

Although proud of his heritage as a descendant of Abraham, Caiaphas did not complain of the opulent home that Rome provided for whoever the Emperor appointed to be high priest. Patterned after the Roman 'domus' architecture, the gate from the street led into a courtyard surrounded by several connected residences, which housed his extended family, including his father-in-law, Annas, who had been high priest before him.

'What do you mean you don't know where this Juda is?' Annas's whiplash tone – and the cringing posture of Caiaphas and the two leaders of the Sanhedrin – illustrated the power the older man still had. Although not openly admitted, Annas retained much influence with Rome. *'Caiaphas may wear the high priest's robes,'* it was whispered, *'but only because Annas said he could.'*

Caiaphas shrugged. 'All I know is that the captain of the temple guard sent a messenger ahead of him,' he said. 'They have arrested Yeshua, but Juda is not with them.'

'If we do not have this Juda,' Annas growled, 'who will provide the testimony needed to condemn the Galilean?'

'Do we really need Juda?' the president of the Sanhedrin asked. 'After all, he thought we merely wanted to talk with Yeshua privately, not kill him.'

'Well, Pilate is not going to execute this man simply because I request it,' Annas snapped. 'Caiaphas, have Yeshua brought to me. I will question him.'

'What will we do?' Caiaphas asked.

'While the president and the father of the court assemble the Sanhedrin,' Annas spoke, as if to a slow-witted child, 'you will try to find this Juda – or *anyone* – who can provide testimony against Yeshua that will satisfy Rome.' He looked at his son-in-law, who was still standing in front of him. Annas waved his hands at the three men, as if shooing chickens, 'Now, *go!*'

The three men glanced at each other and then, nodding to Annas, walked through the courtyard and out into the night.

Annas turned to a servant who was hovering nearby. 'Bring my chair to the small garden outside my home,' he said. 'I will receive the Galilean there.'

By the time the temple guards escorted Yeshua to the villa, a chair made of gleaming acacia wood was set on the other side of a short wall that separated Annas's home from the common courtyard of the domus.

The captain of the temple guard ushered Yeshua to stand in front of the chair. 'Leave three men here,' he said to his second-in-command, 'and position the rest of the guard around the villa. We must be prepared in the event that the prisoner's followers decide they are men and try to free him.'

After several minutes, the door to the residence opened and Annas stepped into the garden. He crossed to Yeshua and circled him, inspecting him as if he were an animal in the market. Then walking over to his chair, the old priest sat down and took a long drink from a goblet placed on a near-by table.

'Inform your men that members of the council will be arriving,' he said to the captain. Then he looked at the man standing before him. 'So, you are Yeshua from Nazareth,' he said. 'I have heard much about you, from many people. But you know how people can spread rumours. So I wan-ted to talk to you – to hear the truth from you.' He steepled his fingers. 'Let's begin with your followers. Who are they? Where do they come from?'

Yeshua looked at Annas, but did not reply.

The older man tried a different approach. 'I have heard that you teach things that are contrary to the teachings of temple leaders and the elders,' he said. 'What have you to say about that?'

'The things I teach are widely known,' Yeshua replied calmly. 'People everywhere have heard me. I teach regularly in the synagogues and in the temple. What I teach in private,

I also teach in public. Why are you asking me this? Ask those who have heard me; they will tell you.'

Yeshua slumped as the captain of the temple guard struck him.

'Watch what you say to the high priest,' the man snarled.

Blood streaming from his mouth, the Teacher straightened and looked at the guard.

'Do you hit a man for telling the truth?' Yeshua said. 'If I said something wrong, tell me what it was.'

The captain raised his hand again.

'Enough,' Annas said. 'Before the night is over, he will have opportunity to answer. Take him to Caiaphas's house.'

The captain grabbed Yeshua's upper arm and jerked him round. He shoved him towards the courtyard. 'Walk!'

Two men hid in the shadows, watching the contingent of guards lead Yeshua across the common courtyard to Caiaphas's house. As the Teacher passed, they looked at each other.

'Cephas,' Yochanan whispered, 'we must follow them. You heard Yeshua. We can testify before the Sanhedrin; we can tell them the truth. He has never said anything about leading a rebellion against Rome.'

'These men don't care about the truth,' Cephas said. 'They want his blood, and ours too if they catch us here. I was *crazy* to let you talk me into coming.'

'You can stay here or you can leave!' Yochanan snarled. 'I'm going in there.' Turning, the younger disciple followed the group of people to the far side of the villa where, in a larger courtyard, a crowd had already gathered.

Cephas looked around and then trudged to the far wall, where a few guards sat near a brazier. He drew near so he could warm his hands by the fire while looking directly into the courtyard.

At the far end, Yeshua stood at the base of the steps that led up to a platform where Caiaphas sat on a stone bench. The crowd – members of the Sanhedrin, as well as many elders and leaders – stood behind the Teacher.

A man dressed in rags stood next to the high priest, facing Yeshua. 'That is the man,' he said, pointing at the Teacher. 'I heard him say we should stop giving to the temple.'

A gasp rippled around the courtyard.

'I see,' Caiaphas said. 'But did you hear him say we should rise up against Rome?'

The man, grinning at the response from his first statement, spoke without thinking. 'No!' he said. 'Only a madman would try to defeat Rome . . . oh wait,' Caiaphas's expression recalled him to his purpose, 'I mean . . . uh . . . I heard him say . . .' he sputtered into silence.

Caiaphas sighed. 'You may go,' he told the man. 'Captain, bring in the next witness.'

'Hey wait a minute! When am I going to get paid?' the man said. 'Ouch!' he cried when the captain of the temple guard grabbed his elbow and roughly escorted him out.

The next 'witness' was not dressed very differently from the first man. When Caiaphas asked whether he had heard Yeshua speak treason, the man nodded.

'Yes, I did,' he said. 'He said that we could belong to another kingdom.'

The men standing around the room murmured to one another.

Caiaphas smiled. 'Did he say *how* this kingdom would come about?' he asked.

The man thought for a moment and then snapped his fingers. 'By being an instrument of YHWH's peace in the world.'

At the back of the crowd someone sneered. Caiaphas stood up to see who was laughing, but Yochanan had pulled his head cloth forward and turned away, slipping into the shadow of a column. The high priest released the witness and called for the next one to be brought in.

'Caiaphas,' Yosef from Arimathea stepped forward. 'I was called out in the middle of the night because this was *supposed* to be an important hearing. I will not take part in the false accusation of this man.'

'Neither will I,' Nicodemus crossed to stand with Yosef.

Caiaphas patted the air with his hands. 'Wait, Yosef, Nicodemus,' he said trying to calm two of the richest men in the Sanhedrin. 'Those two men were here by mistake.'

On the other side of the courtyard, Cephas was trying to hear what was happening in the trial.

'You were with Yeshua.'

Cephas spun round to see a servant girl pointing at him. She held a tray with cups of wine for the soldiers around the brazier. 'You are one of his followers. I've seen you with him,' she said.

Cephas looked at the girl and then at the soldiers. Several of the men set their cups down and rose, drawing their swords from the leather sheaths. He shook his head wildly. 'I do not know him,' he stuttered.

He stood up and walked to where another group of men stood near a window opening to the larger courtyard. They were intent on listening to the trial and did not see Cephas join them.

'He said that he could destroy YHWH's temple,' a third 'witness' told Caiaphas. Looking around at the temple leaders and elders who did not respond to his outrageous testimony, the man added, 'H-he also said, "Once I destroy it, I can rebuild it in three days."'

From the bored expressions of the Sanhedrin – as well as their feet shifting on the marble floor – Caiaphas could tell he was losing control of the proceedings. Standing, he asked Yeshua, 'Don't you have something to say for yourself? Aren't you going to answer any of these charges?'

Yeshua looked at him and said nothing.

'Sir, would you like a cup of wine?'

Cephas turned to see another servant girl standing near him. Her eyes grew wide. 'Lela was right,' she said. 'You were with Yeshua from Nazareth! I saw you the other day, when he entered Jerusalem.'

The curse that flew out of Cephas's mouth startled him as well as those standing near. 'I do not even know this man!' he snarled and stomped off to stand near the brazier by the gate of the courtyard. This time Cephas could not escape his questioners, as a small group of people followed him.

'Didn't I see you with him in Gethsemane?' a man asked. 'There was a man with your build who cut off the ear of the high priest's servant.'

'By the living God,' Cephas yelled, 'I do not know Yeshua.'

Cephas froze horror as the crow of a cockerel announced the coming dawn. When the bird squawked again, he remembered, '*Before the cockerel crows twice, you will deny me three times.*'

Cephas turned towards where the sham of a trial was taking place. From where he was, he could see Yeshua – his friend, his Teacher – gazing straight at him. The pain of betrayal in Yeshua's eyes cut to Cephas's heart like a knife.

Hot tears blinded his eyes. As he stumbled from the high priest's courtyard, Cephas heard Nicodemus's voice.

'Caiaphas, this hearing does not abide by the Law!' Nicodemus announced. 'According to our Law, you cannot try a man under the cover of darkness.'

'You want a legal hearing?' the high priest asked. 'As you wish! Captain of the guard, take the prisoner to the temple. Now that it is day, Yeshua the Galilean will officially be tried before the Sanhedrin.'

* * *

The captain of the temple guard escorted Yeshua from the home of the high priest, past Herod's palace, to the temple. Once inside, he led Yeshua to the magnificent chamber that was the official meeting room of the Sanhedrin. The members of the council were seated in a semi-circle, with Caiaphas in the centre, when the guard brought Yeshua into the room and stopped in front of the high priest.

After staring at the Teacher for several minutes, Caiaphas stood up and spread his arms wide.

'We are assembled to determine the guilt of Yeshua of Nazareth,' he said. 'Since all of you have heard the testimony against him, this is a mere formality.'

'Caiaphas,' Nicodemus said, 'while we were at your house, we did not hear any evidence to convict Yeshua of anything.'

The high priest lifted his hands in surrender. 'You're right,' he said. 'We would not want to sentence anyone unjustly.' He turned to Yeshua. 'We have been told that you are considered to be the Messiah.'

'If I tell you, you will not believe,' Yeshua said, 'and if I ask you a question, you will not answer.'

Caiaphas opened his mouth and then stopped. He couldn't afford to lose control now, this was too important; he clenched his fists and took a deep breath.

'I charge you,' he said to Yeshua, 'by the name of the living God, to tell us whether you are the *Messiah*, the Son of YHWH.'

Yeshua looked straight at the high priest. 'I AM,' Yeshua's voice resonated with power and authority. 'It is as you say. There will come a day when you will see me, sitting at YHWH's right hand and returning on the clouds of heaven.'

The high priest's scream of anger pulled everyone's eyes back to him. Grasping the neck of his priestly robe, Caiaphas pulled, ripping the garment. 'He has blasphemed!' he screamed. 'Do we need any further evidence? What do you think?'

The president of the council stepped forward. 'Why would we need to hear any more testimonies?' he cried. 'With his own mouth he condemned himself.'

'He deserves death!' the father of the court shouted.

The cry was repeated throughout the chamber. 'He deserves death! He deserves death!'

The high priest walked down the steps and crossed to stare at Yeshua. Suddenly he slapped the Teacher.

The action released waves of rage in the chamber. Some of the council members stepped forward to spit on the Teacher, some slapped him and others hit him with their fists.

'Stop this!' Yosef cried. 'This is not right!' He and Nicodemus were restrained by two temple guards.

'You cannot beat this man,' Nicodemus said, struggling against the guard who held him.

'They are right,' Annas said. He walked up to Yeshua, who had fallen to the floor, his face bruised and bleeding.

Annas held a long narrow piece of cloth in his hands. 'Here, captain,' he said, handing the cloth to the captain of the temple guard, 'you know what to do with this.'

The guard looked at the priest and then smiled grimly at the cloth. He grabbed both ends and wrapped it around Yeshua's eyes, tying it at the back.

When the beatings resumed, each slap, each blow was followed with a taunting, 'Prophesy to us, *Messiah!* Who hit you that time?'

When the beatings finally stopped, the captain jerked Yeshua – bruised and bloodied – to his feet.

'Yeshua ben Yosef,' the high priest said, 'the penalty for your blasphemy is death.' Turning to the captain, he said, 'Take him to Pilate. I will speak with the Governor. He has the authority to carry out the death sentence.'

The captain and the temple guard led Yeshua out of the chamber. The members of the council followed soon afterwards, each man going to his own home to prepare for the next day of the Passover celebration. While Annas, Caiaphas and the Council leaders were congratulating themselves on the successful proceedings, a man startled them when he burst into the room.

'Juda,' Caiaphas breathed in relief. 'Where have you been?'

'You lied to me,' Juda gasped. 'That was not the plan. You were going to talk with Yeshua. Convince him to lead a rebellion against Rome.'

'*We* had *other* plans,' Caiaphas said. 'Why are you complaining? You were well paid.'

'Don't you understand?' Juda screamed. 'I betrayed an *innocent* man!'

Caiaphas shrugged. 'What is that to us?' he asked. 'That is your responsibility, not ours.'

Juda ran to the door of the chamber, where he stopped. Reaching into his robe, he pulled out a bag and poured out coins into his hand.

'I am not the only one responsible for his blood!' he cried and threw the coins across the room. Thirty silver coins clattered and spun on the floor. Turning, he ran out of the temple, his cry, 'I am not the only one responsible for his blood,' echoing through the courts of the temple.

'You there,' Annas said to a young temple guard. 'Go after him and bring him back here.' As the guard left, the older priest explained, 'If he goes to Pilate, he could ruin all our plans.' He turned to the president of the Sanhedrin and the father of the court. 'You two wait here and deal with Juda. Caiaphas and I will go and state our case to Pilate.'

The temple leaders sat down to wait for the guard's return; they spent the time discussing the evening's events. When the young guard stumbled back into the court, his face was ashen. 'He's gone,' the man gasped.

'What do you mean, *gone*?' the president asked.

'Juda's dead,' the guard stuttered. 'He hanged himself.'

'He committed suicide?' the father of the court gasped.

'There's more,' the man swallowed. 'The rope he used was old, very old.

After he . . . died . . . the rope snapped. His body fell and,' the man gulped, 'burst open, spilling his guts . . . all over the rocks.'

'Enough,' the president said. 'We understand.' As the guard left, he turned to the other man. 'What will we do with the money he threw into the temple? It is blood money; it would be improper to put it into the temple treasury.'

'Wait,' the father of the court said. 'The potter's field is for sale for thirty pieces of silver. We can buy the field and use it to bury strangers.'

'Good,' the president said. 'Well, that takes care of Juda. Soon, all this will be behind us and the world will forget all about Yeshua the Galilean.'

* * *

On the north side of the city, a soldier looked at the two temple leaders standing at the foot of the steps leading to the Antonia Fortress.

'What do you want?'

Caiaphas opened his mouth, but Annas spoke first.

'Tell Governor Pilate that Annas and his son-in-law, High Priest Caiaphas, must speak to him immediately.'

The soldier stared at the two men and then stepped aside. 'Come in,' he sneered. 'I'll inform the governor that you're here.'

Caiaphas opened his mouth, but Annas once more interrupted him. 'It's Passover. If we enter the house of a

Gentile, we will be . . . *ceremonially unclean* . . . and will not be able to celebrate the remainder of this week's festival. Pilate knows our ways; he will understand,' he said.

The soldier did not reply; he merely nodded his head and walked into the depths of the Antonia Fortress. A while later he returned, followed by Pontius Pilate, the fifth Roman governor of Judea.

Dressed in the blood-red tunic and gleaming breastplate of a Roman soldier, with a short sword strapped to his side, Pilate greeted the two priests with a simple nod.

'It is Passover week. You must want something *special* to come here at this time,' his voice was oily. 'Please tell me how Imperial Rome may help you.'

'We have sent the temple guard to you with a prisoner. His name is Yeshua ben Yosef.'

'A prisoner?' he sneered, clearly bored. 'What is your charge against this man?'

Both priests opened their mouths, but Caiaphas spoke first.

'We would not have brought him to you if he were not a criminal,' he retorted.

'Ah, so you can speak faster than your father-in-law,' Pilate smiled. 'I don't have time for your petty religious disputes. Take him and try him yourself.'

He turned to go back into the fortress.

Caiaphas placed a foot on the bottom step. 'Only the Romans are permitted to execute someone,' he said.

Pilate turned around. 'You want me to *execute* someone during one of your religious festivals? What did this man do?'

'He perverted our nation and forbade people to pay the tax to Caesar,' Caiaphas said. 'He claimed to be the Messiah, the King of the Hebrews.'

Pilate looked at the two priests. 'Israel doesn't have a king,' he said. 'Rome did away with the Jewish kingdom.'

'This man claims to be the Messiah. According to our prophecies, he is supposed to rule on King David's throne.'

Pilate thought for a moment. Then he nodded. 'I will see him.'

Turning, he walked down the halls of the fortress to the chamber he used as his office. It was starkly furnished with a simple desk and several chairs. A fire burning in a small brazier took the morning chill out of the air. Lamps with polished brass mirrors placed behind provided sufficient light by which to study reports.

While he waited, he picked up a stylus, dipped it in a small pot of ink and made notes on several reports. The echo of feet marching down the corridor announced the approach of the soldiers and their prisoner.

The door opened and a soldier stepped into the room and saluted. 'The prisoner is here.' He stepped aside as two soldiers – with a man between them – entered the room.

The man, dressed in a simple robe, was still bloodied from the beating he had received at the temple. His face was bruised and his eyes were nearly swollen shut.

What did this man do that the priests would beat him so? Pilate thought. Throwing his stylus on the desk, he looked at the man. 'You are Yeshua ben Yosef?' The man didn't reply, but nodded his head. 'So, are you this . . . *Messiah* . . . the King of the Hebrews?' Pilate asked.

Yeshua looked at the Roman. 'Is this your own question,' he asked, his voice weak, 'or did someone else tell you about me?'

'I am not a Hebrew,' Pilate said. 'How would I know about the Messiah? Your own priests brought you here. Why? What have you done?'

'I am not an earthly king,' Yeshua answered. 'If I were, my followers would have fought for me when I was arrested. My kingdom is not of this world.'

'Ah, so you admit that you are a king, then?' Pilate asked.

'You are right in saying that I am a king,' Yeshua said. 'I was born for this purpose. I was born to bring truth into the world. Everyone who loves the truth recognizes that what I say is true.'

'Truth?' Pilate laughed. 'What is truth?' The governor stood. 'Wait here,' he told his soldiers. He walked out of the fortress to where the two priests were waiting for him. 'I have questioned this Yeshua,' he said. 'He is not guilty of any crime.'

'He has challenged the rule of Rome and yet you say he is not guilty of any crime?' Annas was incredulous. Seeing their chance of destroying the Galilean slipping away, Annas and Caiaphas began to spit out any accusations they could think of against Yeshua.

'He stirs up the people,' Annas said, 'teaching throughout Judea, from Galilee to Jerusalem.'

'He is a Galilean?' Pilate asked. 'Well, then, he is under King Herod's rule.' Turning to the soldier at his side, he said, 'Send the prisoner to Herod.'

* * *

Yeshua was dragged through the streets of Jerusalem like a rabid dog. His every step was followed by crowds of people. Blood trickled down his face and from his wrists. Eventually they approached Herod's palace.

'Yeshua from *Nazareth*?' Herod smiled arrogantly when the messenger handed him Pilate's note. 'I have heard many reports about him. Who knows, maybe he will perform a miracle.'

Sitting down, he nodded to the servant. 'Bring in the prisoner.'

A moment later, Annas and Caiaphas, along with the guards escorting Yeshua, entered the room.

After greeting the chief priests, Herod said, 'I understand that you want me to question this man.'

Herod's hope of witnessing a miracle was unfulfilled. The chief priests stood shouting about all the things they claimed Yeshua had said and done. Herod questioned the prisoner yet, despite question after question, Yeshua refused to answer Herod and remained silent.

Bored and angry for having his time wasted, Herod began taunting Yeshua. 'We must honour our prestigious visitor,' he sneered. Turning to a soldier, he said, 'Help the King of the Hebrews to a seat.'

'Certainly,' the soldier saluted Herod. Turning towards Yeshua, he bowed. 'Would *Your Majesty* please be seated?' Sticking out a booted leg, he kicked Yeshua's feet, knocking him to the ground.

Laughter erupted all around.

'He must be dressed like a king,' Herod laughed. 'Here,' he said, picking up his robe and tossing it to the soldier.

The soldier caught the robe while another dragged Yeshua to his feet. He wrapped the robe around the Teacher's neck and then stepped back.

'Behold the King!' Herod announced.

'Behold the King!' the soldiers laughed.

The priests joined in the laughter, mocking Yeshua, who stood in the middle of the room, his blood staining the rich fabric and the purple of the robe reflecting the bruises on his face.

When Herod realized that Yeshua was not going to speak or entertain them with a miracle, he instructed the soldiers to send the prisoner back to Pilate.

'Tell him I don't care what is done with the King of the Hebrews.'

* * *

Later that morning, the solider dragged Yeshua back into the Antonia Fortress, to a chamber where Pilate was reading over morning reports.

'Sir, Herod returned the prisoner Yeshua,' the soldier announced.

Pilate looked up. 'What? Did he not try the man?'

'No,' the soldier said. 'From what I was told, Herod thought the prisoner could perform some sort of "magic" for entertainment. When he didn't, Herod and his soldiers ridiculed him.'

'What?' Pilate said. 'Is Rome the only country that understands justice?'

'Sir, there is something more,' the soldier said.

'What is it?'

'As he was escorted through the city, the prisoner drew a crowd. They followed him here. They are waiting in the large courtyard to hear your judgment of the prisoner.'

'They want judgment do they?' Pilate rubbed his chin. 'Isn't today the day for that strange custom when I release any prisoner the people want?'

The solider nodded. 'Yes, I believe it is, sir.'

'Who else do we have in the prisons?'

'Barabbas.'

'Isn't he the one charged with rebellion and murder?'

'Sir, you're not thinking of releasing Barabbas?' the soldier asked.

'No, but the priests don't have to know that,' Pilate said. 'I'll bring both men out and let the people choose. No one in their right mind would choose that murderer over this *Teacher*.'

Walking to the large courtyard in the Antonia Fortress, Pilate found the area packed with Hebrews, young and old, rich and poor. He recognized servants of the priests, wandering through the crowd. They were speaking to people and – here and there – the sun caught the glint of coins they were handing out.

A moment later, the soldier brought Yeshua out to stand next to Pilate. Dressed in the bloodied royal robe, exhausted from beatings and going without food, water or drink through his many trials, the Teacher swayed as he faced the crowd.

The crowd roared with anger when they saw him.

Pilate stood and raised his hands to silence them. 'Your priests brought this man to me. They claim that he perverted the people and tried to turn them against Rome. I have questioned him and cannot find any evidence to support this accusation and neither could Herod. He has done nothing to deserve death, so I will flog him and then release him.

'Or,' Pilate added, 'I can follow your old custom and release a prisoner to you. Who do you want, Yeshua, who is called the Messiah, or Barabbas the murderer?'

The crowd was silent for a moment and then, from the back, came a voice, 'Give us Barabbas! Give us Barabbas.' The person was too far away for Pilate to identify the voice, but soon the crowd picked up the chant, 'Give us Barabbas! Give us Barabbas.'

Pilate waved the crowd to silence. 'What about this man, this Yeshua, who is called the Messiah? What should I do with him?'

From another corner of the crowd came the cry, 'Crucify him!' The hatred in the voice surged through the crowd, who began chanting, 'Crucify him! Crucify him!'

'Why?' Pilate shouted over the chanting crowd. 'He has done nothing wrong.'

But the deadly chant continued, 'Crucify him! Crucify him!'

Pilate turned to the soldier at his side. 'I don't know why, but these people want to see this Yeshua bleed.'

'What should we do?' the soldier asked.

'Flog him,' Pilate said. 'Perhaps thirty-nine lashes with the flagrum will satisfy their blood lust.'

The soldier saluted and turned to issue the order. Within minutes, Yeshua's hands were chained to a pole and his clothing removed. Two soldiers – one thickset, the other tall and muscular – stood on either side of him, holding the flagrum, a multi-tailed whip with pieces of metal and bone tied into the leather lengths. When a person was flogged with one of these whips, the pieces of metal and bone would snag into the flesh, ripping skin and muscle as the soldier jerked back the whip. The men selected to wield the flagrum were known to enjoy inflicting pain, and loved hearing men scream under its deadly touch. Many men did not survive such a flogging.

The first lash of the whip from the thickset soldier caught Yeshua's shoulder, ripping a long, bloody gash down his back. The second lash from the taller soldier caught his legs, gouging his thighs. He cringed and moaned as the flogging continued. The blood made the stone pavement around the pole slick and Yeshua would often slip in his own blood. The flogging lasted for thirty-nine cruel lashes.

By the time it was over, Yeshua was slumped against the pole. He moaned when the soldiers unbound his hands.

'Ah . . . he's still alive,' the thickset soldier laughed as he jerked the Teacher upright.

Yeshua groaned, shivering with the pain.

'Oh look,' said the tall soldier, 'the King of the Hebrews is cold.' He grabbed Herod's robe that had been removed before the flogging and wrapped it around the bleeding man. 'Here's your royal robe, *Your Majesty.*'

The thickset soldier walked to a thorn bush growing in a corner of the courtyard. He pulled out his sword and cut a long branch from the bush. Quickly stripping off the leaves, he twisted the branch into a circle. He walked to where Yeshua was being held upright by his other torturer.

'A king must have a crown,' the soldier said. He placed the circle of thorns on Yeshua's head and then pressed it down.

Yeshua groaned as the thorns pierced his forehead. The blood dripped from the wounds into his eyes and down his face.

'Don't forget a sceptre,' the tall solider said.

The thickset soldier looked around and crossed to where a long wooden staff, thicker than a man's thumb, was leaning against the wall. Carrying it back, he knelt before the bleeding Messiah and offered him the staff.

'Here is your sceptre, *Your Majesty.*' Straightening, he lifted the staff and swung it, hitting Yeshua's head. Both soldiers thought this great fun and took turns striking the 'King of the Hebrews'.

'Come on,' the thickset solider said. 'It's time to show you to your people.'

They dragged Yeshua back to the large courtyard. Gasps and screams erupted from the crowds when they saw the bloodied body of the Teacher.

Pilate forced himself to breathe deeply to keep from vomiting. Then he stood before the crowd.

'Look at him!' he cried, pointing to Yeshua, 'I want you to know that I have found no fault with this man.'

Pilate looked out over the crowd, now shocked into silence. Out of the corner of his eye, he saw movement. Turning his head, he saw several priests whispering to people in the crowd, nudging others.

'Crucify him!' came the weak cry again, to be taken up and repeated until the chant echoed throughout the courtyard.

'What has he done that you hate him?' Pilate asked.

'He blasphemed,' one man yelled. 'He claimed to be the Son of God.'

'The Son of God!' The soldiers whispered fearfully to each other.

Romans were raised to believe in a large number of gods who frequently took on human form to walk among men. When angered or crossed, these gods rained down fearsome judgment. If they had tortured and mocked the son of a god, who knew what retribution they would face!

Pilate walked up to Yeshua. The Teacher's eyes were closed and every breath began and ended with a moan.

'Where do you come from?' Pilate asked. When Yeshua didn't respond, he asked, 'Why won't you speak to me? Don't you know that I have the authority to release you or the power to crucify you?'

Yeshua opened swollen, bruised and bloodied eyes. 'You would have no authority over me,' he whispered, 'if it were not given to you from heaven.'

Shaken, Pilate turned back to the crowd. 'Isn't flogging this man sufficient?' he asked. 'Why do you still want him to die?'

'You are a Roman,' Annas cried out. 'If you release this man, you are betraying Caesar! For we have no king but Caesar!'

Pilate whispered to a servant who left and returned moments later carrying a basin of water. Dipping his hands, he washed them.' I am innocent of the blood of this man,' Pilate said. 'If he is killed, it is by your hand.'

'Let his blood be upon us,' someone cried, 'and upon our children!'

Pilate looked out over the crowd screaming for blood and then turned to his soldiers. 'Release Barabbas to them,' he said.

'What should we do with Yeshua?' one soldier asked.

'Give them what they want,' Pilate whispered. 'Crucify him.'

25

The Execution

Cephas stumbled through the morning light, not heading in any direction, just running, each step accenting memories that haunted him.

'I would die for you!' . . . *'Before the cockerel crows twice, you will deny me three times'* . . . *'I do not know him'* . . . *'I do not even know this man'* . . . *'By the living God, I do not know Yeshua!'*

Cephas had always considered himself to be a bit of a 'Samson' – strong and mighty in the face of all foes; now he realized he was a coward who'd abandoned his closest friend. After the nightmare in the courtyard of Caiaphas, he had wandered the streets of Jerusalem, trying to forget, yet knowing he would never forget. By the time the approaching dawn washed the morning sky with pinks and yellows, he had found a gate out of the city and run.

Soon, he looked up to see the outline of Bethany. He paused. Eleazar and his two sisters were hosting many of the followers of Yeshua for Passover. He started to change direction, but then stopped. Clenching his fists, he wrestled with himself. Finally, he turned and resumed walking towards Bethany.

They will hate me for the rest of their lives, he thought. *But they need to know about Yeshua.*

Walking past the burial place where Yeshua had called Eleazar back to life, Cephas turned up the road that led to Eleazar's house. He stepped up to the door and knocked. It didn't surprise him to hear voices through the door. Marta would have been up long before now in order to prepare enough food to feed her guests.

When Mayrim opened the door, she looked at him in surprise, and then threw herself against his chest, weeping.

'Cephas!' she cried. 'I'm so glad you're safe. Come in.' Grabbing his hand, she pulled him indoors where, to his surprise, the remainder of the Twelve – now the Eleven – were gathered. In the corner of the room, Yochanan and Yaakov sat next to their mother, along with Miriam from Magdala and . . . Miriam, Yeshua's mother. From the painful wide-eyed expression on their faces, Cephas realized that they had heard what happened.

'Sit down,' Mayrim said, pushing him towards a low table. 'Marta, Eleazar!' she called, 'Cephas is here!'

Her brother and sister entered the room carrying trays of food. Eleazar explained how, one by one, the other disciples had showed up during the night, Yochanan arriving a short time before Cephas.

'We heard how the temple guards . . . arrested . . . the Teacher,' Eleazar lowered his voice with a glance towards Yeshua's mother. 'It must have been horrifying for all of you, trying to get away, so you could find help for Yeshua.'

Cephas's eyes opened wide in surprise as he glanced around the room. From the expressions on the other disciples' faces – each man avoiding looking at the others, bright spots of red staining their cheeks – he realized that no one had told the whole story about what had happened in the garden.

Eleazar continued, 'Yochanan arrived shortly before you did and said that the Sanhedrin had . . .' he took another quick glance at Miriam, '. . . condemned Yeshua and had sent him to Pilate.'

'Eleazar is not without influence,' Marta said, grasping her brother's arm. 'The Sanhedrin does not have the authority to carry out a . . .' She paused and looked at Yeshua's mother. 'Forgive us, Miriam, we don't mean to wound you with our words.'

'Do not apologize,' the Teacher's mother said. 'I understand that you want to help my son. I know you love him as much as he loves you.'

Guilt twisted Cephas's stomach and he fought down the bile rising in his throat.

'There are many of Yeshua's other followers here and in Jerusalem,' Marta continued. 'We will go to Jerusalem and try to speak to Pilate on the Teacher's behalf. We will convince him that Yeshua is innocent of the accusations the priests brought against him.'

Cephas nodded hesitantly, but did not respond. The rest of the Twelve were silent as well. As the women bustled around the room, offering food and discussing plans, hopelessness welled up inside him. *Even if the impossible could happen and Yeshua was set free*, he thought, *he would never forgive us. We all betrayed him, just as he said.*

* * *

The small band of disciples heard the noise before they reached the slope leading into Jerusalem. People lined the road from the city gate. The crowd was wild; some people were screaming, others crying. Fights broke out here and there; Roman soldiers patrolling the multitude settled the fights with a curse and a quick clout on the head with a sword hilt.

'Eleazar, what is happening?' Marta asked.

'I don't know,' he answered. 'I cannot see over the heads of the people in the crowd.'

Marcus, one of the young men following Yeshua, ran over to a tree on the side of the road and quickly climbed up to a thick overhanging branch.

'Roman soldiers are leading someone – no . . . there's more than one person – down the street.' He gasped. 'They're carrying crosses.' He looked down at Yeshua's followers, his eyes wide with shock. 'They're crucifying prisoners today!'

'Crucifixion!' Marta gasped. 'Who could it be? The Romans only execute the worst of criminals by crucifixion.'

'I heard they were going to crucify Barabbas and two of his men,' Eleazar said. 'It sounds like the crowd are calling for their blood.'

Marcus climbed down the tree. 'Barabbas and his band may be murdering thieves,' he said, dusting off his robe, 'but I pity anyone who has to endure crucifixion. The Romans have perfected that as a terrible form of execution.'

'What are we going to do?' Mayrim asked. 'We need to speak to Pilate soon and this road is the fastest way to the Antonia Fortress.'

'Well, we can either wait for this crowd to leave or we can go to one of the other gates,' Cephas said.

'Let's go to the other gate,' Marta said. 'Even if he is a criminal, I don't want to see Barabbas – or any of his men – having to carry their own cross out to be killed.'

Cephas started to reply, when Miriam from Magdala screamed.

'What is it?' Marta asked.

Mayrim lifted a trembling finger towards the gate. 'It's *Yeshua*!' she gasped.

The disciples spun round.

Yeshua – their friend and their Teacher – was staggering under the weight of an enormous rough-hewn cross. From head to foot, his body was a mass of bleeding wounds, staining the purple robe he wore. As he took a step, he collapsed, falling to the ground, the cross striking his head, shoving the thorns he wore in a parody of a crown deeper into his flesh.

'Nooo!' Yeshua's mother ran down the road where a Roman soldier was beating her son with the side of his sword.

'Miriam, stop!' Yochanan ran after her and grabbed her arms.

'Let me go, Yochanan!' the older woman was wild with grief, trying to jerk free from his grasp. 'What are you doing? He is my son; he is your cousin! We must save him!'

'Miriam, *Miriam!* Listen to me!' Several people in the crowd were glancing their way and he pulled the struggling woman to the shadow of the tree Marcus had climbed. 'We are too late. Yeshua is carrying a cross; that means that Pilate has already rendered his judgment.' Tears filled his eyes. 'There is *nothing* we can do.'

Yeshua lay panting on the street, blood dripping from his face onto the stones. He cried out when a lash from the short whip held by a Roman soldier stung his bloodied back.

'Get up!' the soldier bellowed.

Yeshua inched fingers along the length of the rough cross until he reached its centre. Grimacing, he balanced the cross and rose to his knees, only to fall again.

The soldier raised the whip over his soldier, but was stayed by a sharp retort from his centurion.

'You fool! Beating him will accomplish nothing,' he said. 'He can barely hold himself up. Find someone to carry the cross.'

The soldier inspected the crowd and then strode over to grab a tall, muscular man. 'You,' he said, 'what's your name?'

'Shimon,' the man said, 'from Cyrene.'

'Well, Shimon from Cyrene,' the solider sneered, dragging him over to where Yeshua lay pinned down by his cross. 'You're going to carry the cross for the King of the Hebrews.'

Shimon looked at the soldier and then at the man lying on the road. He bent over, picked up the cross and placed it on his dark, strong shoulder.

The soldier grabbed Yeshua and pulled him to his feet. Yeshua swayed for a moment, eyes closed, as he drew in ragged, shallow breaths. Then he opened his eyes and looked at Shimon.

'Thank you,' he whispered. He shifted his body as if carrying a burden no one could see and stumbled up the road.

Outside the city walls was the area used by the Romans for crucifixions; the people living locally called it 'Golgotha' (the place of the skull). It was close enough to the main road that people coming and going from Jerusalem would see the condemned men dying and be reminded of the penalty for crimes against the empire. The ground bore the marks of previous crucifixions, and here and there were traces of blood from earlier victims.

Yeshua was the last of the condemned men to arrive. By the time he stumbled to a standstill, with Shimon beside him bearing the cross, the Romans were securing the other two men to their crosses.

Piercing screams echoed across the hill as tapered iron spikes – as much as seven inches in length – were driven into the area beneath the fleshy part of their palms. Then the soldiers secured each prisoner's feet to the cross by laying their feet one on top the other with a single spike driven through them.

Three Roman soldiers approached Yeshua. One walked up to Shimon and pulled the cross from his shoulders; it fell to the earth with a dull thud. 'Thank you,' the soldier sneered scornfully, 'you've been most helpful.' Shoving Shimon out of the way, he turned to Yeshua.

'Now it's your turn, *Your Majesty.*' He grabbed the neck of the Teacher's robe with both hands and started to pull.

'Don't tear it,' a second soldier said. 'Herod gave this robe to him. You see the trim around the neck and sleeves and hem? That's made of gold thread. We are allowed to divide up the prisoner's belongings. Even bloodied, that piece would be worth something.'

After the soldier had slipped the robe from his shoulders, Yeshua fell to the ground, gasping for air.

The soldiers positioned the cross between the other two crosses and kicked the foot of the cross until it was in the right place to be erected later when the innocent victim was securely nailed to it. After grabbing a hammer and a thick metal spike, they walked back to the cross . . . and froze.

Turning over, Yeshua reached a hand out to take hold of the cross. He was pulling himself on top of the post, moaning as rough splinters pierced his already wounded flesh. When he reached the cross beam, he shifted his body and laid his bloodied back against the cross. Grimacing, he extended first his right hand and then his left along the rough wooden beam.

The soldiers stared at the bloodied man. He had offered himself up to be crucified!

'I've served Rome for over thirty years,' said one of the soldiers, 'and I've never seen that happen before.'

'It's almost as if he *wants* to die,' the other whispered.

'Are you not done yet?' the centurion demanded. 'Hurry up! I don't want to be out here a single minute longer than I have to.'

'Get the wine that's mixed with myrrh,' the older soldier said. 'It drugs the prisoners and reduces the pain.'

The young soldier brought a jug filled with wine. He knelt by the cross, lifted Yeshua's head and put the jug to his bruised lips. When he tasted the wine, Yeshua closed his mouth and turned his head away.

'He doesn't want it,' the young soldier said.

The old soldier grunted. 'All right then, if he wants to suffer, he'll suffer.'

Two of the soldiers knelt by each end of the cross beam and the third soldier at the foot of the cross. Laying Yeshua's hand against the wood, one of the soldiers placed the point of a thick spike against his wrist. The soldier lifted the hammer over his shoulder and brought it down on the head of the spike, driving the metal again and again through Yeshua's flesh. Too weak to scream, Yeshua moaned, writhing from the pain. The other soldiers drove the spikes through his other hand and his feet.

The old soldier walked over to the centurion and came back carrying a flat piece of wood. He placed it above Yeshua's head and, picking up another spike, hammered it onto the cross.

The soldiers looped several long lengths of rope around the cross beam. Taking hold of the ends of the rope, they pulled, jerking the cross upright until it was jolted into place with a flesh-ripping shudder.

'How long does it take them to die?' the young soldier asked.

'It depends,' the old soldier shrugged. 'Could take most of the day, could take several days. In the meantime, I've brought along a fresh jug of wine and some dice.'

The centurion passed nearby as the younger soldier said, 'But I didn't bring any coins.'

'We don't gamble for coins,' the centurion laughed. He reached down to pick up the discarded robe. 'We gamble for the prisoners' clothes.'

The soldiers passed around the dice and the jug. The soldiers didn't care who won the ragged clothing of the two thieves. They consoled the young soldier who 'won' the rags, laughing over the stench wafting from the cloth. When they came to the robe Yeshua wore, however, the gambling grew serious. Though soaked with blood, the cloth was valuable.

The hours passed to the sounds of the groans of the men on the crosses, fighting off death under the weight of the merciless Judean sun.

* * *

'Centurion!' Caiaphas pushed his way through the crowd surrounding the crosses to where the soldiers were dividing their winnings.

The centurion rolled his eyes as he stood to face the high priest. 'What is it?' he asked.

'What is the meaning of this?' Caiaphas turned to point at the sign nailed above Yeshua's head. Written in Aramaic, Latin and Greek, it read:

Yeshua from Nazareth; the King of the Hebrews

'What is the meaning of this?' the high priest screeched. 'It shouldn't say, "King of the Hebrews" but "This man claimed to be King of the Hebrews." I will take this up with Governor Pilate!'

'Pilate said you might question the sign,' the centurion said. He pulled a rolled scroll from inside his breastplate and handed it to the priest. 'He also said this note would answer your *concerns.*'

Frowning, the high priest took the scroll and peered at the wax seal before slipping a thumb under the seal to break it. He unrolled it and scanned the message. Suppressing a curse, he tossed the scroll on the ground and stomped away.

The centurion picked up the discarded roll and read it before sputtering into laughter.

'What does it say?' the old soldier asked.

The centurion grabbed the jug of wine and took a deep drink. 'It says, "*I meant exactly what I wrote!*"'

Pilate's betrayal infuriated Caiaphas. He stomped to the foot of the cross and looked up at Yeshua. Sneeering he said, 'Look at you now. You claim you can destroy the temple and rebuild it in three days? You must be the Messiah. Well then, prove it; save yourself and come down from the cross.'

Annas walked up to stand next to his son-in-law. He turned to face the crowd of people staring at the dying men.

'He saved others,' he scoffed, sweeping a hand towards Yeshua, 'but he cannot save himself. He claimed to be the Messiah, the Son of YHWH. Let him come down from the cross and we will believe in him.'

Yeshua looked down at the priests at the foot of the cross, sneering and scoffing. He pressed on his nailed feet while pulling up on his arms to lift himself up enough to fill his lungs. 'Father,' he rasped, 'please forgive all of these people; they don't know what they are doing.'

'Hey! Hey you!' the thief hanging on the left side of Yeshua moaned as he pushed up on the nail piercing his feet. 'If you're the Messiah then prove it! Save yourself and save us too!'

'You're dying,' the thief on the right side of Yeshua wheezed. 'Don't you even fear YHWH?' He pushed up to fill his lungs. 'We deserve to die for the things we have done.' Another shallow breath. 'But this man hasn't done anything wrong.' Groaning, he pushed up on his pierced feet once more and then turned to look at the man on the cross between them. 'Yeshua, please remember me when you come into your kingdom.'

Yeshua's expression softened as he looked at the thief. 'I promise that today you will be with me in paradise.'

'Yeshua!'

The Teacher looked down to see his mother standing next to his cousin and disciple, Yochanan.

Seeing her son – the child she had carried, the son she loved – bruised, bleeding, pierced and dying, Miriam collapsed in Yochanan's arms, wailing.

'Mother,' Yeshua whispered. He pushed up to fill his lungs. '*Mother*! Think of Yochanan as your son.' Another breath. 'Yochanan, care for her as you would your own mother.'

Holding the Messiah's weeping mother, Yochanan looked at his cousin and teacher, his throat working to hold back tears. He nodded and then, turning, gently coaxed Miriam to walk away from the sight of her dying son.

The sky, which had been bright with the noontime sun, suddenly grew dark. The centurion called for torches, but they could not fight the inky blackness. For three hours, the sky remained dark as midnight.

'*Eloi! Eloi! Lama sabachthani?*' Yeshua's cry – suddenly full and strong – echoed through the darkness.

'What did he say?' the young soldier whispered. 'It's Aramaic, but I don't understand the language.'

'It means, "My God, my God, why have you forsaken me?"' the centurion whispered. For the first time that day, he sounded shaken.

Someone in the crowd shouted, 'Listen, did he just call for the prophet Elijah? Let's see whether the prophet comes to take him down from the cross.'

'I'm thirsty,' Yeshua whispered.

The young soldier crossed to where a bucket and some sponges were placed near the crosses. The bucket was filled with wine vinegar to be given to the prisoners. Dipping a sponge in the bucket, the solider placed it on a long pole and held it up to Yeshua.

When he had taken this drink Yeshua looked at the people mocking him at his feet. He looked at the soldiers, who had stopped gambling and were staring at him. He lifted his head and looked to where his disciples stood weeping. He looked beyond, as if staring into eternity. Then pushing on his feet, Yeshua filled his lungs one last time.

'It is finished!' he shouted. '*Father*, I give my spirit into Your hands!'

Lowering his body, Yeshua dropped his head to his chest and died.

A groan began deep in the earth as the ground beneath the crosses began to shake. Rocks exploded, shooting deadly shards into the air. The earthquake ran from Golgotha into Jerusalem. Some buildings swayed with the shifting earth; other buildings crumbled into debris. The walls of the temple shook and cracked, and in the Holy of

Holies, the veil of the temple – the thick curtain that separated the presence of holy YHWH from sinful man – was ripped in half from top to bottom.

Chaos reigned at Golgotha. Priests and soldiers screamed and held each other, crying out in fear. Others ran, trying to dodge the flying debris. Holding on to the base of the cross for support, the centurion looked up; he had seen enough death to know that Yeshua was gone.

'Truly, this was the Son of God!' he exclaimed.

26

The Resurrection

Yosef of Arimathea approached the centurion and handed him a scroll. 'I have permission from Governor Pilate to bury the body of Yeshua ben Yosef.'

The officer split the wax sealing the scroll and scanned the message. Then he turned to two of his soldiers, 'Take the body down and give it to this man.'

Several people stood near the foot of the cross while the soldiers lowered the bloodied body of Yeshua. Nicodemus had brought a litter to carry the body. Miriam from Magdala and Miriam – the wife of Cleopas, Yeshua's father's brother – held baskets with cloths and jars of water to wash the body as well as clean linen to wrap it in.

As the two men placed Yeshua's battered body onto the litter, Nicodemus said, 'It is nearly sunset; we must put the body in a tomb quickly.'

'Come,' Yosef replied, 'I know where there is a new tomb we can lay him in.'

'A new tomb?' Yeshua's aunt cried hysterically. 'He must not be buried alone; he must be cleaned and anointed and buried with those he loved! How could I face his mother if I left his body alone?'

'Be at peace, Miriam,' Yosef said. 'Today we will honour Yeshua by washing his body and wrapping it in fine linen. After the Sabbath, we will return with the burial spices and perfumes.'

'All will be done to honour Yeshua,' Miriam from Magdala said, wiping away tears with the edge of her head cloth. 'I will come early the morning after the Sabbath and do what needs to be done for him.'

The tomb was a cave in a garden near Golgotha. Yosef helped Nicodemus roll the massive stone from the hole that formed the tomb's entrance. Lighting a lamp, Yosef crawled in and then turned round to help Nicodemus slide the litter through the opening. The two women and then Nicodemus crawled into the hole.

Once inside, the tomb was tall enough so that they could stand with no problem. Hewn into the stone there was a ledge at waist height – wide enough to hold a body – with narrow niches carved into the cave wall above.

Nicodemus and Yosef moved Yeshua's body from the litter to the ledge. Then, from the back of the chamber, they began chanting from the Holy Scriptures.

The two women washed the body, weeping over the wounds and bruises the dirt and blood had covered. They prepared a mixture of myrrh and aloes, smoothed it over the body, and then wrapped it with the strips of linen. Before leaving, Miriam took a length of cloth and gently laid it around Yeshua's head. With a final prayer, the group left the tomb.

After Yosef and Nicodemus had rolled the stone in front of the opening, they escorted the two women to Eleazar's house where the mourners were already gathering. Miriam from Magdala made plans to return to the tomb on the morning following the Sabbath to continue the burial rituals.

* * *

In the Antonia Palace, fear and concern walked before the Pharisees.

'Caiaphas. Annas,' Pilate greeted the temple leaders. 'I am surprised to see you today. Isn't today still part of the Passover celebration? Is there someone else you want Rome to crucify?'

Caiaphas opened his mouth, but Annas replied first. 'No,' he snapped. 'We understand that you gave the body of the criminal, Yeshua ben Yosef, to some men for burial.'

Pilate's smile was thin and cruel. 'Yes, I did,' he said.

'Who did you give it to?' Annas demanded.

Pilate arched an eyebrow at the priest's tone. 'Yeshua is dead,' he snapped.

'Are you certain about that?' the high priest asked.

'My soldiers reported that you were at Golgotha mocking Yeshua. Surely you saw him die.'

'Surely you were aware of the sudden earthquake that occurred yesterday,' Caiaphas said. 'We had to return to the temple. We needed to arrange for the temple guards to protect it lest someone took advantage of the darkness and tried to steal some of its treasures.'

'But we did send someone back to instruct the soldiers . . . to . . . hasten the criminals' death,' Annas said.

Pilate nodded. 'Ah yes, I heard about that from my centurion. Something about not desecrating the Sabbath. My soldiers broke the legs of the two thieves to prevent them from pushing up on their feet; death comes soon thereafter.

'But it was unnecessary in Yeshua's case; he was already dead.'

'How can you be certain?' Annas asked.

'To confirm it, one of the soldiers took a spear and stuck it through the side of Yeshua's chest. Blood and water poured out of the wound.' Pilate took a deep breath. 'I've seen enough death. Let me assure you, Yeshua is dead.'

'Where is he buried?' Caiaphas asked.

'Isn't it enough for you that he is dead?' Pilate asked. 'Haven't you done enough to him?'

Caiaphas touched his father-in-law's arm to stop him from exploding in rage. 'Governor,' Caiaphas said. 'This morning Annas and I remembered a story we had heard. Apparently, while he was alive, Yeshua told many people that three days after he died, he would rise again. We ask that you give an order for his tomb to be made secure to prevent his disciples from stealing the body and telling everyone that he rose from the dead. That deception would be worse than any other.'

Pilate sighed. 'All right,' he nodded. 'I will learn where the body is buried and arrange for the tomb to be sealed and a guard to be posted.'

'And your men are trustworthy?' Caiaphas asked. 'Would they accept bribes?'

Pilate's face grew dark with anger. 'First, you demand that I crucify a man I believe to be innocent,' he said. 'Then you *suggest* that my men would take money to tell lies?'

Annas spread his hands, shrugging his shoulders. 'My son-in-law is not *suggesting* your men would lie,' he said. 'As we said earlier, we are merely trying to protect the people from more lies.'

* * *

For all that the temple leaders hated Yeshua, there were people who loved him. They gathered together to watch the dark hours. The next day was a Sabbath like none they had ever known. Fearful that the temple leaders might come for them next, they did not go to the synagogue.

'Will the dawn ever come?' Miriam said. 'We must go back and finish preparing Yeshua's body.'

'I cannot believe he is dead,' Marta whispered, wiping away tears. 'How could this have happened? What are we going to do now?'

'We will go back to doing what we used to do,' Cephas said. 'I was a fisherman before; I'll be a fisherman again.'

'"*Come with me*,"' Yochanan whispered, '"*from now on, you will catch men for YHWH's kingdom.*"' He looked at the others. 'Do you remember when he asked us to be his disciples?'

Levi smiled slightly. 'He came up to me at the tax collector's booth, and just said, "*You. I want you to come with me and be one of my disciples.*" I had never met him before, but I just got up from the table and left.' He shook his head. 'I've never regretted it since.'

'He healed me,' Miriam from Magdala said. 'I was sick with so many illnesses. I was in constant torment. Yet he came and commanded the illnesses to leave.'

The family and friends of Yeshua spent the rest of the day sharing memories of everything Yeshua had said and done. Every now and then, the room would grow quiet as they remembered the torturous death he had endured. Then someone would break down, sobbing, and soon, the room would be filled with the sound of heart-wrenching grief.

'We'll never see him again,' Mayrim wept.

'I'll never be able to thank him again for what he did for me,' Eleazar said, tears running down his beard.

Cephas got up and walked outside to the courtyard. Climbing the stairs that led to the roof, he stared up at the sky, his throat constricting with unshed tears.

'I would die for you!'

'Before the cockerel crows twice, you will deny me three times.'

'I do not know him . . . I do not even know this man . . . by the living God, I do not know Yeshua!'

'Aiiiii!' Cephas fell to his knees, groaning. Placing his hands on his head, the big fisherman began to rock back and forth, weeping. 'I'm sorry, Yeshua!' he cried. 'I'm so sorry.'

* * *

The morning sky was washed in golden hues when Miriam from Magdala and Yeshua's aunts, Salome (mother of Yaakov and Yochanan) and Miriam, entered the garden where Yeshua's tomb was. They carried baskets filled with myrrh and aloes.

'I woke this morning, hoping this was all a nightmare,' Salome said. 'When I saw my two sons sleeping on Eleazar's floor,' her voice caught on a sob, 'I realized it was true. He's gone.'

'At least we can honour him in death,' Miriam wife of Cleopas said. Then her eyes widened. 'I just remembered, the stone! It is too big for us to move. What will we . . .'

'Look!' Miriam from Magdala gasped.

The area around the tomb was littered with rocks, branches and fallen trees, as well as two discarded Roman swords. Then they noticed the stone rolled away from the entrance of the tomb.

'What happened?' Salome whispered.

The other women couldn't answer; they shook their heads.

Suddenly angels appeared before them. Taller than any giant, they radiated with a glow that made the morning sun look dim. Screaming, the three women dropped their baskets and fell to their knees, pressing their faces to the ground.

'Why are you looking for the living among the dead?' the angels spoke as one. 'He is not here; he has risen. Remember what he told you when he was still with you, "The Son of YHWH will be killed and after three days, will come back to life."'

'Come and see the place where he lay.'

* * *

Not long afterwards, the three women burst through the door of Eleazar's house screaming.

'Cephas! Yochanan! Andros! We've seen *Him!* We've seen Him!'

The men jumped up. Cephas ran to the entrance to see whether anyone was outside and then turned to hear the remarkable story the women told.

'*Angels* told you that Yeshua is still alive?' Yochanan asked.

His mother nodded. 'And as we were leaving the garden, there was a man standing in front of us. *It was Him! It was Yeshua!*'

Mary from Magdala took up the story. 'His clothing was brilliant white, like the angels'. And he greeted us.' She laughed. 'We fell at his feet worshipping YHWH. Then Yeshua told us to come and tell all of you to go to Galilee and he would meet you there.'

Cephas and Yochanan looked at the women and then, turning, they ran out of the house. They ran the two miles from Bethany to the tomb near Golgotha.

Yochanan arrived at the garden tomb first. No one was there, not a Roman soldier nor an angel. He bent over and looked inside: the morning light illuminated the interior of the tomb. He could see the linen strips, but there was no sign of a body.

Cephas arrived a moment later, still breathing hard from running. The two men looked at each other and then entered the tomb.

'Look, here are the linen strips they wrapped around him,' Yochanan said. 'What have you got?'

Cephas lifted a folded piece of linen. 'This is the cloth that they put over his face. Who would stop to fold a cloth?'

'Don't you understand?' Yochanan started laughing. 'If someone came to steal his body, they would have to defeat the Roman guard, break the seal and carry the body away before anyone returned. If caught, they would incur the death penalty. They wouldn't stop to remove the linen strips and fold the head cloth.

'Don't you see what this means, Cephas?' Yochanan grinned. 'Yeshua is alive!'

* * *

'So let me understand this,' Caiaphas said. 'Two large angels flew down out of the sky, scaring you so badly that you fainted. And when you woke up, the stone had been rolled away from the tomb and the body of Yeshua was gone?'

The soldiers looked at each other and then at the high priest; they nodded.

'And why did you come to us?' Caiaphas asked.

'Because Pilate wouldn't believe us and would have had us put to death,' the older soldier said.

'You were wise to come to us first,' Annas said. 'We will be glad to help you, but you are going to have to help us.'

'How?'

'You are to tell anyone who asks, "We fell asleep and the disciples came and took the body.'

'What if the story gets back to Pilate?'

'Don't worry about Pilate,' Annas said. 'We will think of something that will satisfy him and keep you out of trouble.' He crossed to a cabinet and took out a large bag that clinked. 'Share these coins with your men,' he said. 'Tell them it is our gift for all the troubles you have gone through on our behalf.'

Caiaphas saw the soldiers to the door and returned to where his father-in-law stood, staring into the lamplight.

'Well, I think we handled that well,' Caiaphas said. 'We have no worries; Yeshua from Nazareth will never bother us again.'

Annas looked at him. 'Do you truly believe that?' he asked. 'I don't know. I have a feeling that, no matter what we do, the power of the name of Yeshua will live long after we are both dead.'

27

Alive!

The two men had walked the seven miles from Jerusalem to Emmaus many times and never failed to admire the beauty of the mountains dotted with trees and shrubs that rose up on either side of the road. Today, they did not notice the spring green edging the trees or the smell of newly opened flowers.

'How can we believe such a story?' Daved asked.

Cleopas shook his head. 'I don't know,' he said. 'But they were so certain – angels, the stone rolled away, Yeshua alive. How can we not believe them?'

Daved waved his hand dismissively. 'They are women,' he said. 'Who believes women?'

'Yeshua did,' replied Cleopas.

Daved stopped walking. He took a deep breath and blew it out. 'You're right,' he said. 'We were raised to believe that women were not to be trusted, but Yeshua always treated them with kindness and respect.

'But Cleopas,' Daved continued, 'he's *alive*? Cleopas, I was there! I'll never forget that day. I watched him suffer for six hours and I saw him die.'

'I know, Daved,' Cleopas whispered, 'I was there too.'

'Greetings.'

The two men looked over their shoulders to see a stranger walking their way. He was of average height and build, and what hair and beard wasn't hidden by his head cloth was dark and wavy.

'May I join you on your journey?' His voice was deep and rich.

'We would be honoured,' Cleopas said. 'I am Cleopas and this is Daved. And you are . . .?'

'A stranger in a strange land,' the man replied with a slight smile.

Cleopas glanced at Daved, but neither man challenged the stranger.

'I understand, friend,' Cleopas said. 'With everything that has happened these last few days, it is understandable that you wish to protect your identity.' His deep sigh was echoed by Daved.

'What are these *happenings* of which you speak?' the stranger asked.

Daved's eyes widened. 'You don't know?' he asked. 'Friend, it is obvious that you were not in Jerusalem this Passover.'

'What happened?' the man asked.

'Yeshua from Nazareth,' Cleopas said. 'He was a teacher and a prophet. His understanding of YHWH and His Law was amazing.'

'And he performed many miracles,' Daved added. 'Healing the sick, giving sight to the blind; he even fed more than five thousand people with just five loaves of bread and two fish.'

'But the leaders of the temple hated him because he accused them of twisting YHWH's Law for their own gain,' Cleopas said. 'They arrested him four days ago. The trial was a sham – with witnesses lying and saying he was trying to overthrow Rome's rule. They handed him over to Governor Pilate who had him . . . crucified,' he whispered. His throat constricted and he wiped his eyes.

The stranger laid his hands on both men's shoulders. 'I am sorry for your loss,' he said.

Daved nodded. 'We had hoped – we had *believed* – that Yeshua might be the Messiah who would restore the kingdom to Israel. And then today, three days after his death, several of the women we know told us an amazing story.'

'What did they say?' the stranger asked.

'They went to the tomb early this morning to anoint the body with the burial spices, but found it was empty!' Cleopas explained. 'They came running back telling us that they'd seen angels who told them Yeshua was alive! They even claim to have *seen* him.'

'Two of our friends – who were also disciples of Yeshua – went to the tomb and found it empty just as the women had said,' Daved said, shaking his head. 'We don't know what to believe. Angels? Yeshua is alive? I want to believe, but *I saw him die*. It just doesn't make sense.'

'Well it makes perfect sense to me,' the stranger said.

The two men looked at him, doubt painting their faces.

'Is it so difficult to believe all that the prophets foretold?' the stranger said. 'Did they not say that the Messiah would have to suffer all these things and then enter into his eternal kingdom?

'Remember what YHWH told Moses, "*I will raise up a prophet like you from among Israel and you must listen to Him. I will tell that prophet what to say and He will tell the people everything I command Him.*" Who better to speak for YHWH than His Son?

'And remember the prophet Isaiah, who said, "*Who has believed our message and to whom has the arm of the Lord been revealed . . . He was despised and rejected by men, a man of sorrows, and familiar with suffering. Like one from whom men hide their faces, He was despised, and we esteemed Him not.*

"*Surely He took up our infirmities and carried our sorrows, yet we considered Him stricken by God, smitten by Him, and afflicted. But He was pierced for our transgressions, He was crushed for our iniquities; the punishment that brought us peace was upon Him, and by His wounds we are healed. We all, like sheep, have gone astray, each of us has turned to his own way, and YHWH has laid on Him the wrongdoings of us all.*

"*He was oppressed and afflicted, yet He did not open His mouth; He was led like a lamb to the slaughter, and as a sheep before her shearers is silent, so He did not open His mouth. By oppression and judgment He was taken away . . . For He was cut off from the land of the living; for the transgression of my people He was stricken. He was assigned a grave with the wicked, and with the evil-doers in His death, though He had done no violence, nor was any deceit in his mouth . . . He poured out His life unto death, and was numbered with the rebellious. For He bore the sin of many, and prayed for the transgressors.*" '

Cleopas and Daved listened wide-eyed to the stranger as he continued to remind them of the words of the prophet and how they had been fulfilled by Yeshua.

'So, he truly *is* the Messiah,' Cleopas said wonderingly. 'But just not in the way we were taught. Thank you, friend, for explaining all of this to us.'

They looked up to see the village of Emmaus ahead, and at the end of the road, Cleopas's house.

'This is the end of our journey,' Cleopas said.

'Then I thank you for allowing me to travel with you,' the stranger said, 'and I wish you well.' He turned and continued down the road.

'Wait,' Cleopas called. The stranger stopped and looked at him. 'It's late. We would be most honoured if you would stay with us for the evening. You can continue your journey in the morning.'

The stranger smiled. 'I would be honoured to stay with you.'

Cleopas hurried ahead to inform his wife that they were to have an extra guest, while Daved waited to escort the stranger indoors.

When the food was placed on the table, Cleopas looked at the stranger. 'I know that as the head of the house I should offer thanks to YHWH. However, you spoke with such insight today; would you please offer thanks instead?'

The stranger smiled. 'Certainly, I will.' He took a piece of flatbread from the dish and lifted it towards the ceiling of the room. 'Father,' he said, 'You always provide for those who love You. Thank You for sending Cleopas to bless Daved and me with his generous hospitality.'

Tearing the bread in half, he turned and handed it to Cleopas. 'Take this bread,' he smiled at him.

Cleopas heard his gasp echoed by Daved. 'Yeshua!' he cried and reached for the Teacher who . . . disappeared.

The men jumped up and searched the room and the rest of the house. Yeshua was not there.

'He's alive!' Cleopas grinned.

Daved grinned back. 'How could we not recognize him?'

Cleopas shook his head. 'I don't know,' he confessed, 'but I do know that when he talked to us about the Holy Scriptures, my heart felt like it was burning inside me.'

'Come!' Daved said, running to the door. 'We must tell the others that Yeshua is alive!'

They hurried all the way back to Jerusalem and on to Bethany, where they found most of the Eleven – Taoma wasn't present – as well as some of Yeshua's other followers.

'It is true!' they cried, laughing. 'The women were right! Yeshua has risen! He appeared to us!'

Cleopas and Daved stumbled over each other's words as they told what had happened on the journey and how they recognized Yeshua when he prayed over the bread.

'He's alive?' Yochanan asked, grinning.

Cleopas nodded. 'He's alive.'

The room erupted with laughter and rejoicing.

'We told you,' Miriam of Magdala smiled.

'Greetings and peace.'

They all turned to see a man standing in the centre of the room.

'Yeshua!'

Some of the women ran to kneel at his feet, followed by Cleopas and Daved. But the others stood back, fearful.

'Is it a ghost?' Levi whispered.

'Why are you afraid and why do you doubt?' Yeshua said. He showed them his hands and feet; the holes from the nails – although no longer bleeding – were still in his flesh. 'Touch me and see; it is me! A ghost does not have flesh and bones.'

Yochanan crept forward – trembling from joy and fear – and peered at the extended hands. He turned round to look at the others and nodded.

'Do you have something to eat?' Yeshua asked.

Marta picked up a dish and carried it hesitantly to him. Yeshua lifted a piece of fish, blessed it and ate it.

'Teacher,' she asked timidly, 'is it truly you?'

He smiled and nodded. 'It is me.'

The room erupted again in excitement. Then, just as he had done with Cleopas and Daved, Yeshua explained how the Messiah must die to fulfil the prophecies. 'It was necessary so that repentance and forgiveness for sins would come to all men.'

He stayed with them for a while longer and then disappeared.

When Taoma returned to the house, instead of finding everyone mourning – as expected – everyone was celebrating.

'Taoma!' Yaakov grasped his forearms. 'We have seen Yeshua.'

Despite what everyone told him, Taoma adamantly refused to believe. 'I'm not saying that you're lying,' he said.

'But I saw Yeshua nailed to a cross and die.'

If you don't believe us or the women,' Cleopas said, 'what will you believe?'

'Until I see the nail marks in his hands,' he said, 'and put my finger where the nails were, and put my hand into his side, I will not believe it.'

No matter what they said, the others could not convince him that their Teacher was alive.

* * *

A week later, the disciples gathered again.

'Lock the door,' Taoma said.

'There is no need,' Andros said.

'There are rumours that the chief priests are looking for us,' Taoma said. He crossed the room and locked the door. Turning around, he gasped.

Yeshua stood in the centre of the room.

'Greetings and peace,' Yeshua said. Turning to Taoma he extended his hands. 'Put your finger here; see my hands. Reach out your hand and put it into my side. Stop doubting and believe.'

Taoma fell to his knees, 'My Lord and my God!' he whispered in awe.

'You believe because you've seen me,' Yeshua said. 'But I tell you, blessed are those who have not seen me and yet believe.'

28

The Fisherman

Cephas crossed the room to stare out of the window. Then he turned and walked back to where the rest of the Eleven were sitting around the low table. The platters held the remains of fish, bread, cucumbers and olives, evidence that the disciples had appreciated his wife's and mother-in-law's cooking. One platter, however, was left untouched. Ruth had insisted that no one should eat a date and honey cake until Yeshua had eaten the first one. Cephas turned and walked back to the window.

The sun was slipping behind the hills on the western side of the Sea of Galilee, casting shades of orange over the waters. Three years ago, when the sun was at this position, he would have been preparing to go out on the sea to fish.

That was before he had met Yeshua and the Teacher had asked him to leave his boat and follow him around the country. For the last three years, Cephas had seen more of Israel than ever before; he had witnessed miracles and he had learned more about YHWH than he had learned in all his life. He had thought – as had all of Yeshua's followers

– that they were going to see the kingdom restored to Israel and that he would be an important person in that kingdom.

That was before that horrible night that began in the upper room.

'Even if everyone else denies you, I never will. I would die for you!' he had vowed.

After running away in fear, he'd sneaked into the courtyard at the high priest's home, where he was recognized as a follower of Yeshua. Rather than admit the truth, he'd spoken the words that would haunt him for the rest of his life.

'By the living God, I do not know this Yeshua.'

To his shame, he'd denied his friend and teacher not just once, but three times.

Like all the disciples, Cephas was crushed when Yeshua was crucified and was overjoyed when Yeshua had been resurrected. But when Yeshua appeared to the Eleven in the upper room, they'd all realized *who* Yeshua was: the Son of YHWH.

'I denied the Son of God!' Cephas berated himself every day.

In those few times that Yeshua had appeared to them, Cephas had not spoken with him alone. *What will He think of me?* the fisherman wondered. *How can He ever forgive me for what I did?*

The day after Yeshua had appeared and showed Taoma His pierced hands and feet, they had all obeyed His request and returned to Galilee. Each morning they were certain He would appear sometime during the day and by the evening they were disappointed by His absence.

These last few days had allowed plenty of time for Cephas to ponder; and he didn't like thinking. A voice intruded on Cephas's thoughts. He turned to look at the other men. 'Huh?' he asked.

'You weren't even paying attention,' Andros sighed and rolled his eyes. 'I *asked* whether you knew what Yeshua wanted us to do?'

'Why would *I* know that?' Cephas snapped.

'Because you always claimed to be one of the Teacher's chief disciples,' his brother retorted.

'Don't fight,' Levi said. 'Yeshua told us to come to Galilee. We've been here for several days and He has not appeared. All we want to know is what we are supposed to do next.'

Cephas looked at the other men in the room and then glanced out of the window at the darkening sky. Making a decision, he slapped his thigh. 'You want to know what to do?' he asked. 'I don't know about the rest of you, but I'll tell you what I'm going to do.'

The other disciples looked at him expectantly.

'I'm going fishing.'

He stood up and wrapped his cloak around his shoulder. Striding to the door, he paused. 'Ruth, I'll be back in the morning.'

He was out of the house and walking down the road when he realized Andros, his brother, together with Yochanan, Yaakov and several other disciples were following him.

Zebedee, Yochanan and Yaakov's father, had maintained the boat belonging to Cephas and Andros. Untying the ropes – wrapped around a large rock to keep the boat from floating away – the men pushed the boat off the beach, and then jumped in. The sails were hoisted and soon they were sailing to their favourite fishing spots.

Although they were a bit rusty at first, it didn't take long before it was as though they had never left the sea. Gathering the nets in their arms, throwing them out onto the water where they sunk to the depths – the old skills had not been forgotten. However, as all men of the sea knew, there were times when the most skilled fisherman, for some unknown reason, did not catch a thing. Throw after throw, hauling in the net to cast it again, even changing location, did not help. By the time the distant hills were barely visible against the early dawn, they had not caught a single fish.

'Let's give up, Cephas,' Andros said. 'I'm exhausted.'

Cephas hated to give up. 'Let's throw the nets out once more,' he said, gathering the wet nets.

'Hello!' a voice drifted through the early morning air.

The men in the boat looked towards shore, where they saw the faint outline of a man standing on the shore. The sun had not risen enough for them to identify the speaker.

Yochanan cupped his hands around his mouth. 'Hello!' he called.

'Friends,' the man called, 'haven't you caught any fish tonight?'

'No, we haven't.'

'Throw your nets on the right side of the boat and you will catch some.'

'Cephas sighed. 'Who is this man that he thinks he can tell me about fishing?'

'A moment ago, you wanted to throw the nets once more,' Andros said. 'Now you want to stop because someone else suggested it?'

Cephas threw his hands up in a sign of surrender. 'All right, all right!' he said. 'We'll throw the nets on the *right* side, as the stranger suggested.'

The men in the boat gathered the nets in their arms and turned to the right side of the boat, where they threw the nets into the water.

As the net slapped the surface of the water, Cephas straightened, crossed his arms and looked at his brother and friends. 'We'll wait a few minutes and then tell the stranger that there are no fish.'

'Cephas,' Andros pointed to the rope from the net; it was taut. 'I think we might have caught something.'

Suddenly, the boat tilted to the side. The men jumped to grab the rope before the boat capsized. When the net reached the surface, it was filled with flopping fish of all sizes and types.

'We've never caught so many fish,' Andros said.

'How did the stranger know?' Yaakov asked. 'The only other time this has happened was when . . .'

Suddenly Yochanan straightened and stared towards the shore. 'It's the Lord!' he said.

Without a word, Cephas jumped into the water and began swimming to shore. Within a few minutes, he was trudging up the shore, water streaming from his clothes. One look confirmed Yochanan's words.

Sitting by a small campfire, where several fish were skewered on sticks and cooking, was *Yeshua*! On top of a flat stone near the fire were several loaves of bread.

Cephas stared at the Teacher without a word.

Yeshua looked at his disciple. 'Bring some of the fish you just caught.'

Cephas nodded and turned. The boat with the other disciples was just reaching shore. Cephas climbed aboard the boat and helped drag the net to the shore. Andros and Yaakov counted the fish while Cephas and Yochanan inspected the net. There were over one hundred and fifty fish and the net was not torn in a single place.

'Friends,' Yeshua said. 'Come and have breakfast.'

The Teacher prayed over the meal and handed it to the disciples. The men ate in silence. Cephas knew the other disciples were wondering the same thing: *Is it truly the Lord?* But he certainly didn't want to be chastised for disbelief.

After the meal, Andros and the other men went back to sort through their catch of fish. Cephas got up to help, when Yeshua spoke.

'Cephas, do you really love Me more than these men?'

The fisherman felt as if he had been punched in his gut. *He is going to condemn me for denying Him,* he thought, swallowing hard. He turned to face the Teacher. 'Yes, Lord,' he said, 'You know that I love You.'

'Take care of My lambs – the young believers. They will need you.'

Cephas didn't say anything, but merely nodded.

'Cephas ben Yochanan, do you truly love Me?'

Sweat broke out on Cephas's forehead. *Why is He asking me again?* he thought. Then he sighed. *Why should He believe me?* He crossed back to sit by Yeshua. 'Yes, Lord, You know that I love You.'

'Take care of My sheep – the older believers. They will need you.'

'I will, Lord,' Cephas whispered.

A moment later, Yeshua asked, 'Cephas, do you love Me?'

Cephas grasped his hands until his knuckles were white. *Why has He asked me this three times?* With a pang he remembered: *I denied Him three times.*

'Lord, You are the Son of God; You know all things. You know that I love You.'

'Feed My sheep with the Word of YHWH. They will all need you,' Yeshua said. And then he continued, 'Let Me tell you something important. When you were younger, you dressed yourself and went wherever you wanted. When you are old, however, someone else will dress you, and you will stretch out your hands and be led where you do not want to go.'

Yeshua smiled at Cephas; the warmth emanating from the Teacher's eyes felt pure as the sunlight that was washing the day. The Teacher grasped Cephas's forearms.

'Come with Me,' Yeshua said. 'From now on, you will catch men for YHWH's kingdom.'

28

The Long Goodbye

'Tell me again, why are we climbing this mountain?' Taoma asked, pausing to catch his breath. Mount Arbel was the tallest mountain around the Sea of Galilee. Walking up its steep face – stark, rocky and pocked with many caves – left the disciples out of breath.

'We are walking up here because the Lord told us to meet Him here,' Cephas said.

'Well, if Lord Yeshua wanted to choose a place that was secluded,' Andros said, panting from the exertion, 'this is a good choice. Few people want to come up here.'

The eleven disciples said little more, but concentrated on placing one foot in front of the other, until they reached the plateau at the summit.

Once there, they admitted that it was worth it. They walked to the edge of the cliff where, with light fluffy clouds dotting the bright blue sky, they were able to see for many miles.

'Greetings.'

Turning, they saw Yeshua standing in the centre of the mountain's plateau.

'Lord!' Yochanan cried, crossing the rocky surface to kneel before Yeshua.

The other disciples dropped to their knees around Yeshua.

'Lord, how wonderful to see You again,' Yaakov said. The others all agreed.

'I confess that sometimes it is hard to believe all that has happened,' Levi said. 'To realize that You *are* truly the Messiah.'

'I agree,' Thaddai said. 'Forgive me, Lord, but all our lives, we were taught that the Messiah would come and restore Israel to the glory of King David's reign. Now I know that is not true; but I'm not sure what to believe.'

'Stand up,' Yeshua said, 'and come here.'

The disciples rose and followed him to the edge of the precipice.

'Look,' he said, sweeping a hand towards the view below. 'Over there, Cephas, I called you and your brother – as well as My cousins Yochanan and Yaakov – to leave all you knew and follow Me.'

Cephas nodded. 'You said that instead of catching fish, we would catch men for YHWH's kingdom.' He shook his head, smiling. 'I confess, I did not know what You meant.'

Yeshua turned to point out another spot. 'There is where a multitude was fed with a young boy's meal.'

'And even though we knew it was a miracle,' Philippos said, 'we didn't understand what that meant.'

'And there,' Yeshua pointed to a spot on the water, 'is where our boat was when the storm rose.'

'I do not know what frightened me more,' Netanel said, 'the storm or the fact that You commanded it to stop.'

'I know,' Yeshua laughed, and the disciples laughed too, each confessing their fears that day.

'I know that, over the past three years, you have each had questions about who I was and what was going to happen,' Yeshua said. 'Now you know who I am.'

'You are YHWH's Son,' Cephas said, his voice filled with awe.

Yeshua nodded. 'I AM,' He said. 'And I know you wonder what will happen in the future.

'My Father has given Me all authority in heaven and on the earth. Now I am sending you into the world. I want you to tell people about Me and about My kingdom. Baptize those who believe – in the name of My Father, in My name and in the name of the Holy Spirit. Love them and teach them everything I have taught you. Those who believe will become part of My kingdom.'

'Will You be with us?' Shimon asked.

'Not for much longer,' Yeshua said. 'Soon, I will return to My Father.'

'But Lord,' Andros said, 'if You were with us, they would believe by the miracles You do.'

'Let Me tell you something,' Yeshua said. 'Anyone who believes in Me will do what I have been doing and, because I am going to My Father, he will do even greater things.

'Do you remember how I commanded demons to stop tormenting people? You – and anyone who believes in Me – will have the authority to do that. You will be able to pray for sick people and they will be healed.'

'This is what the prophet Isaiah spoke about,' Yochanan whispered, his eyes wide, 'when he prophesied, *"Then will the eyes of the blind be opened and the ears of the deaf unstopped. Then will the lame leap like a deer, and the mute tongue shout for joy."*'

Yeshua nodded. 'Yes. And he also said, *" 'You are My witnesses,' declares YHWH, 'and My servant whom I have chosen, so that you may know and believe Me and understand that I am He.'"*

'Come,' Yeshua said. 'We must go to Bethany. There I have something important to tell you.'

They left the next morning. Yeshua led them past the village to the top of the Mount of Olives. As he had done on Mount Arbel, Yeshua crossed to a point on the mountainside where the whole city of Jerusalem was spread below them. He pointed out different parts of the city, reminding them of the things that had happened there, including his death on the cross and the resurrection.

'Do not leave Jerusalem,' he told the Eleven, 'but wait for the gift My Father promised, which you have heard me speak about. For Yochanan the Baptizer baptized with water, but in a few days, you will be baptized with the Holy Spirit.'

'Lord,' Levi asked, 'what about the kingdom? Are You going to restore the kingdom to Israel soon?'

'It is not for you to know the times or dates the Father has set,' Yeshua said. 'But what you may know is that you will receive power when the Holy Spirit comes. You will be My witnesses in Jerusalem, and in all Judea and Samaria, and to the ends of the earth.

'And know this, *I will never leave you*, but be with you – in your spirit – until the end of time.'

Yeshua stopped and looked at each of the Eleven, nodding and smiling.

Then he began to rise above them.

The disciples gasped, as Yeshua – their friend, their Teacher and now their Lord – rose into the sky. They watched, straining their necks, until a cloud moved under Yeshua, hiding him from their sight. They continued scanning the sky, for a sight of him, until a voice spoke.

'Men of Galilee . . .'

The disciples looked down to see two men standing in front of them. They were taller and broader than any man they had ever seen before. From each strand of their hair to every inch of the massive bodies filling their robes, every part of them was a brilliant white.

'Why do you stand here looking into the sky?' they spoke in unison, their voices sounding like the rushing of many waters. *'Yeshua has been taken from you into heaven. But rejoice! For He will come back in the same way you have seen Him go into heaven.'*

YHWH
The Flood, The Fish
& The Giant

*Ancient Mysteries
Retold*

*G.P. Parker
& Paula K. Parker*

From the depths of time come stories that have been told and retold for thousands of years. Now we again have the chance to delve into those ancient mysteries. *YHWH: The Flood, The Fish & The Giant* will take you in to a long-forgotten world.

Twenty stories from the Bible are told by G.P. Taylor and Paula K. Parker in a fresh and exciting way which will open your eyes to the wonders of the Old Testament.

978-1-86024-800-9

Authentic

We trust you enjoyed reading this book from
Authentic Media Limited. If you want to be informed
of any new titles from this author and other exciting
releases you can sign up to the Authentic Book
Club online:

www.authenticmedia.co.uk/bookclub

Contact us
By Post: Authentic Media Limited
52 Presley Way
Crownhill
Milton Keynes
MK8 0ES

E-mail: info@authenticmedia.co.uk

Follow us: